I0761584

About a Place in the Kinki Region
Sesuji

About a Place in the Kinki Region

Sesuji

New York

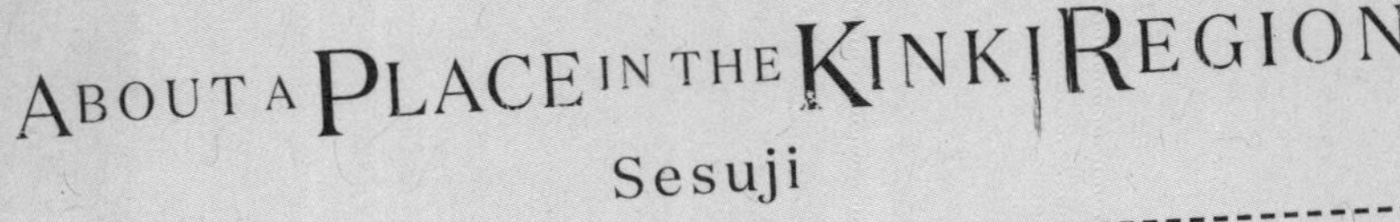

Sesuji

Translation by Michael Blaskowsky
Cover photo by CURBON

KINKI CHIHO NO ARUBASHO NI TSUITE

Yen On
150 West 30th Street, 6th floor
New York, NY 10001

Visit us at yenpress.com • facebook.com/yenpress • twitter.com/yenpress • yenpress.tumblr.com • instagram.com/yenpress

First Yen On Edition: December 2025
Edited by Yen On Editorial: Emma McClain
Designed by Yen Press Design: Andy Swist

Yen On is an imprint of Yen Press, LLC.
The Yen On name and logo are trademarks of Yen Press, LLC.

The publisher is not responsible for websites (or their content) that are not owned by the publisher.

Library of Congress Cataloging-in-Publication Data is available.

ISBNs: 979-8-8554-0994-9 (hardcover)
979-8-8554-0995-6 (ebook)

10 9 8 7 6 5 4 3 2 1

HJM

Printed in South Korea

About a Place in the Kinki Region

Sesuji

Please contact me if you have any information that could help.

Published in July 2017 in a Supplementary Issue of a Certain Monthly Magazine

Short Story: *A Peculiar Comment*

A, a twenty-four-year-old office worker living in Tokyo, joined a software development company straight out of college as an engineer. Once he settled in and got used to the work, however, he found that his days passed by slowly and without much excitement.

With no girlfriend and no hobbies, A surfed the internet to unwind.

"It's kind of embarrassing to admit, but I went to porn sites. I know it's not exactly legal, but there are tons of free places that host videos from the paid ones. Anyway, I got in the habit of checking those sites every day before going to bed."

He even had a favorite one.

"It pirated and reposted new videos from popular production companies, and I went there pretty often. The layout was kind of unique… Most websites recommend content under the frame that plays the video, but this one had a comment section."

A added that his assumption regarding this layout was pure speculation based on his background as an engineer.

"These kinds of websites operate in a legal gray area, and they might have to suddenly shut down one day. So the administrators don't put much effort into the actual site itself. They typically just adapt some framework from another site because it's easier than building everything from scratch. So I suspect the comment section wasn't built by the company operating the site—it just came with the framework they borrowed. I mean, what weirdo wants to start chatting in the comments after watching pirated porn?"

Backing up his claim, the comment sections were mostly empty, aside from the rare complaint like *The video cuts off halfway* or *Upload something new instead of this old crap.* Those remarks never got a response from the site's administrators, either, so it was unlikely the feature was meant to be used.

But one day, A stumbled across an unusual comment.

"It was under the debut video for a new actress from one of my favorite companies. I was really excited to find it, and after watching it, I scrolled down for some reason and saw the comment."

You're very cute. Would you like to come to my place?

"At first, I just figured some old guy who didn't understand how the internet works accidentally commented on the video. But something about it felt off, and it stayed with me."

A month or so later, A found another new video on the site featuring the same actress.

"I watched it, thinking it was pretty quick for her to be putting out a second video. And then I noticed this one had a comment, too."

Please come to my place. I have persimmons.

"My gut told me it was the same person. Obviously, no actress is going to read the comments on a site like this. The whole thing was weird, and it kind of unnerved me."

After that, every time a new video featuring the same actress was uploaded to the site, A would find a similar comment. Since most of the comment sections were totally empty, the strange messages were easy to spot.

"I started looking forward to them, and whenever there was a new video with that actress, I'd check the comments."

That continued for several months. Eventually, the site uploaded another video featuring the actress in question, and the following comment was posted:

Come to the mountain. I have persimmons.

A's boss had yelled at him at work that day, and according to A, a dark curiosity took hold of his mind.

"I figured I'd play a little prank."

So A replied.

Come to the mountain. I have persimmons.

Thank you for always commenting on my videos! This is ○○ [the actress's name]. Where do you live?

Simply posting the reply was enough to satisfy A. He went to bed and completely forgot about what he'd done.

But later, when he saw a new video featuring the same actress, he remembered. There was a comment below the video.

Why haven't you come? I've been waiting for a long time.

"I panicked and went back to the previous video, the one where I'd replied to the guy's comment. He'd answered me."

Come to the mountain. I have persimmons.

Thank you for always commenting on my videos! This is ○○ [the actress's name]. Where do you live?

●●●●●-●●-●●●. *[Redacted because it is a real address.]*

"It included his street number and everything. I couldn't believe he was that serious. It dawned on me that I'd gotten involved with a real weirdo."

Unnerved, A looked up the address on a map.

"I wasn't intending to do anything. I just wanted to see where this weirdo lived."

The location shocked him.

"It wasn't a house—it was a shrine. Not only that, it was a really old one way out in the boonies. I checked the street view, and it showed the place. It was on a little mountain. There was a beat-up torii gate next to the road at the base, with stairs leading up to the shrine grounds. Even the main building was run down, so I figured the place was abandoned.

"I didn't want anything more to do with it, so I stopped going to that website. But for whatever reason, I did check back once. It just so happened a new video with that same actress had been uploaded..."

And beneath the video was the following comment:

Be my bride.

Published March 14, 1989, in a Certain Weekly Journal

A True Story! New Developments Regarding a Missing Girl in Nara?

The same day the Kansai region saw its first snowfall in years, a little girl went missing…

Five years have passed since that day in February 1984 when eight-year-old K from Nara Prefecture disappeared on her way home from school. She still hasn't been found. Regular readers of this magazine will be quite familiar with the story, as well as our editors' efforts over the years to explore numerous possible explanations. There are a slew of suspicious circumstances surrounding her disappearance, and we've looked into a variety of scenarios, from kidnapping by some pervert all the way to UFO abduction. But none of these theories has ever evolved past mere speculation.

However, thanks to exclusive information uncovered during our research, we'd like to propose a new possibility.

As our readers are likely well aware, the unnatural conditions surrounding K's disappearance make this incident particularly strange.

The day she went missing, K was on her way home from school with fellow second-graders Y and E. K's house stood at the end of a cul-de-sac in a busy residential area, while Y and E lived a short walk away. K said her goodbyes and turned down her street, but she never made it to her front door, only forty meters away.

In addition to her own, there were four other houses on K's cul-de-sac, all belonging to families or elderly couples. According to the police investigation, it is unlikely any of them were involved in this case. In other words, at some point while walking those last forty meters from the corner to her front door, K simply disappeared.

None of the houses on the cul-de-sac, including K's, showed any signs of trespassing either inside the home or out in the yard. What's more, K vanished at four PM, when plenty of people were out and about, but no witnesses ever came forward. Numerous daytime talk shows discussed it as a modern case of being spirited away.

The media traded theories, ultimately placing the blame on someone in K's own family. The intense pressure drove the accused to commit suicide a mere two months later, making the case even more memorable.

But now, after years without any new developments, some interesting information has come to light.

• Paranormal Experiment

From nine PM to ten PM on July 13, 1988, ○○ TV aired a program called *The Power of TV: Special Searches for Missing Persons*, which discussed various missing persons cases live on-air and asked viewers to provide any information they might have.

The show included information on K. They devoted a good amount of time to the case, not only sharing details and asking viewers for information, but also inviting an American psychic called ○○○ to Japan for a spiritual reading aimed at uncovering the victim's location. The paranormal experiment used a picture of K, along with maps of both Japan and the Kinki region. Following the reading, the psychic appeared visibly flustered as they gave their report.

"I hate to say this, but I believe K is no longer alive. That said, when the subject of a reading has passed, their picture usually appears faded to me, yet K's is still clear. This has never happened before. The best answer I can give you is that K is not alive, but she's also not dead."

The reporter then asked about K's location, and the psychic pointed to the ●●●●● area inside ●●●●● in the Kinki region. The spot indicated was very far from K's house, and her mother insisted that K had never been there, nor had anyone else in her family.

The hosts said they would have members of their staff investigate that area but ultimately determined no solid leads had been provided during the program. The show never mentioned the case again.

• A Strange Experience

Following our most recent special feature on this story, readers flooded our offices with letters. Our editors found several containing similar testimonies, and we'd like to share those here. The first comes from I, a long-haul trucker.

******

I have to drive all night for my job, and one time I was near ●●●●● around three AM.

The area is pretty deserted. The highway runs between a mountain and a dam, and while there are a handful of houses around, it's very quiet at night, except for the sounds of a few trucks like mine traveling through the pass. There aren't many streetlights, so I have to turn on my high beams.

That night, just as I got to the pass, I saw a girl in a pink sweater with a backpack. She was standing there on the side of the highway, her back to the road.

I figured something bad must have happened, so I pulled over and got out. I walked up to her, but she just kept staring at the woods up on the mountain. Most people turn around if someone walks up behind them. But she didn't.

That's when I started wondering if she might be a ghost. But if she was a real girl, I couldn't leave her there. So I walked closer and asked her if she was okay, if something had happened. That was when I saw her face.

She was smiling. Grinning from ear to ear. She looked up at me with just her eyes, that huge smile still on her face. I was so scared that my knees went weak. But I managed to ask, "Where do you live? What's your name?"

And without the slightest change in expression, she answered.

"I'm K, and I'm gonna be a bride."

I didn't know what to do, but I asked if she'd get in my truck so I could take her home. The next thing I knew, though, she dashed off into the woods. That's right. Straight into the darkness.

I was scared to death. I couldn't follow her. Naturally, I called the police. They took my statement because they had to, but they also asked me if I had been drinking. They were so calm and matter of fact the whole time, like they were used to this kind of thing.

Later on, I saw a missing poster for K outside my local police station. Her name and outfit were exactly the same as those of the girl I saw. I contacted you because no one else would believe such a strange story.

******

In addition to I's testimony, we received several other reports that more or less boiled down to this: "My friend saw a child who looked like K around the ●●●●● area." They all happened at night, and everyone saw K near the ●●●●● area. In many instances, the witness ran away without speaking to her, or K disappeared before they had a chance to say anything.

• The Relative's Death

Near the beginning of this article, we noted that one of K's relatives committed suicide two months after she went missing. The media reasoned he was driven mad after being unfairly blamed by certain unscrupulous reporters for K's disappearance. However, the information we received from those involved contradicts that theory.

The news simply reported that one of K's relatives had committed suicide, noting it as part of the tragedy surrounding her disappearance. We know, however, this relative was M, K's uncle on her father's side.

To begin with, M did not live with K's family. He stayed in a dormitory in Nara owned by the construction management company he worked for, and he only met K's family about once every couple of months. M visited K's house about three weeks before K went missing—he had dinner with the family that day, but they weren't especially close.

Another interesting piece of information about M is his company specialized in dam management, including the ●●●●● dam in the ●●●●● area. M, a management engineer, was assigned to the ●●●●● dam in January.

He left no will behind.

Considering all this, our team believes that M was somehow involved in K's disappearance. This assumption lacks sufficient supporting evidence, however, and so remains mere speculation. We will continue our investigation in the hopes of revealing the truth behind this incident.

About a Place
in the Kinki Region
1

Hello. My name is Sesuji. Thank you for reading this story. Well, I'm not sure if *story* is the right word for it, but thank you for reading this collection of short articles and other pieces.

I'm a freelance writer living in Tokyo. Sesuji is the pen name I'm using for this project; I use a different one for my main work.

I mostly write for horror and paranormal magazines, though sometimes I contribute to radio programs and local TV shows dealing with horror stories. I used to work as an editor for a small publishing house and have spent twenty-odd years in this corner of the industry. But at the end of the day, those subjects will always be a niche interest, so I've recently begun taking whatever work I can get, such as for magazines about dining or gambling. It puts food on the table, so I can't complain.

Some readers might find this sudden interjection by the author jarring. But what you're about to read, which includes my own personal story, will prove crucial to your progress through the book. And once you have understood everything, I would like to ask for your cooperation.

That is why I created this book, so I hope you will read to the end.

My friend has gone missing, and I would like you to provide me with any information you might have.

* * *

I should start by explaining that I did not write the articles appearing in this book.

Nor did Ozawa, my friend who disappeared.

I simply collected a series of articles and snippets from a certain magazine released by the publisher my friend works for (or used to work for), along with some other sources, then I bundled them all together under the title *About a Place in the Kinki Region.* This book contains numerous stories related to a specific place. To be precise, I am talking about an area encompassing multiple locations within the Kinki region, hence the title of this book.

That place spans several prefectures, so its name varies depending on the location. But you could circle the entire area on a map without lifting your pen.

I will provide more details later, but I have decided it's unwise to disclose the precise location. So the name of any spot mentioned in the story that falls inside this zone will be written as ●●●●●.

I met Ozawa, my friend who is now missing, four years ago, just before the coronavirus ravaged Japan.

It was at an in-person meetup for an online community of horror-story fans. Not only am I a horror enthusiast myself, but I find such events useful to source ideas for work, so I often attend them.

This particular group was interested in horror movies, and I remember our small group met at a café in Koenji to discuss the topic.

Ozawa came with his then-girlfriend (he told me they broke up a couple of months later). She liked horror movies and he loved all movies, including horror. A naturally inquisitive person, he listened attentively to what the other members were saying and eventually struck up a conversation with me, as I happened to be seated next to him. He was friendly and a very good listener, and after a while, our conversation strayed from movies. I began telling him the horror stories and urban legends that I had run across throughout my career as a writer.

He was in his second year of university at the time, and I remember being surprised at how fun it was to talk with him, despite our nearly two-decade difference in age. After the meetup, he and I would sometimes update each other on our lives via social media.

One year ago, he sent me a DM.

Long time no type! I started a new job at a publishing company in the spring, and they assigned me to a department that does a magazine on the paranormal! Since that's right up your alley, I had to let you know. It's been a while, and I'm sure there's a lot I can learn from your experience, so I thought I'd invite you for a drink. How about it?

We met up for the first time in several years, and I could tell he'd matured. He already looked like a working adult. I felt like a parent seeing their child all grown up, even though it was only the second time we'd ever met face-to-face.

Nestling into an *izakaya* I frequent in Nakano, we toasted our reunion and caught each other up on recent events. Then he told me about his new job. As it happened, I had written a couple of pieces for that very same company. It's a midsize publisher focused on books and magazines.

"I was looking for a job as an editor of literary works, but they assigned me to a different department… Either way, I got the job, so I intend to make the best of it."

He had been assigned to his publisher's mook editorial department. For those who don't know what a mook is, it's a portmanteau of *magazine* and *book*. If they're associated with a regular magazine, they might also be called "supplementary issues." Essentially, the word refers to these one-off editions, as well as anthologies of articles or comics commonly sold at convenience stores. Ozawa was now working as an editor for this kind of publication.

"Of course, since I'm still a fresh graduate, they didn't want me to work on an issue all by myself. So I started out just shadowing my bosses and running errands."

Then one day, a senior employee presented him with an opportunity.

"Editors usually spend a couple of months on each book, but since I'm new and still helping out on various projects, they said I could work on something of my own over the course of a year. By the way, do you know the magazine called ○○○○ that we publish?"

The magazine he'd named was a monthly publication focused on the paranormal that was quite famous in certain circles.

Though it began as a column in a weekly entertainment news journal called OOOO, it eventually expanded into its own magazine and was a long-running mainstay in its genre, in print for over two decades.

It published a surprisingly wide-ranging assortment of articles, including authentic creepy stories, reports on paranormal hot spots, urban legends, unsolved mysteries, and even UFO sightings. Somewhat surprisingly, this wide breadth of content proved popular with readers, and many paranormal and horror enthusiasts are still devout fans of the magazine. Unfortunately, a downturn in the publishing industry a few years back forced it to stop publication and dissolve its editorial department. Afterward, it hung on to life as a mook, published as so-called supplementary issues at irregular intervals, or occasionally as a convenience store book under a different name.

I had written a few pieces for the magazine at the start of my freelance career and even received some work for the supplementary issues after regular publication ended. They hadn't given me anything recently, but Ozawa's first assignment was to edit the next supplementary issue.

While I didn't say this to Ozawa, I understood his boss's thinking. Times had changed, and a magazine specializing in the paranormal was never going to fly off the shelves. The people buying it would likely be die-hard fans or curious folk just looking for something to kill time, so it would make for a good practice project for a newbie. According to Ozawa, the magazine didn't have a designated editor and the publishing house simply assigned the job to anyone in the mook department who could meet the publication date. It obviously wasn't bringing in much revenue.

Despite all this, he seemed excited to be working on something of his own.

"I suggested going out to paranormal hot spots frequented by horror-related YouTube channels and mixing in interviews with some of the more famous streamers, but…"

His boss rejected the whole idea. I could easily guess why.

"He said reporting and new material like that costs money. And while it would probably make for better content, it's a newbie's job to create good work while keeping costs as low as possible."

The reason sounded plausible enough, but I could tell the publisher just didn't want to waste their budget on the project. In fact, the most recent supplementary issue of the magazine in question had clearly been pieced together using back issues. Every single article induced a feeling of déjà vu, and even an outsider like me could tell the magazine was determined to spend as little money as they could paying third parties.

"Creating something with no budget means I have to use articles that have already been published. But this is my first assignment, so I want to do the best I can."

To my surprise, he had decided to comb through every past issue, including every article from back when the magazine was only a column in a weekly journal. That would mean hundreds of issues, maybe more. But Ozawa had a curious mind, and this was his first job. It seemed he was more than ready to put in the effort required.

"In my downtime, I hole up inside the company archives and read. There's a lot of research material in addition to the old magazines, but everything is crammed haphazardly inside cardboard boxes with no organization whatsoever. So it's going to take a lot of time to check through everything. For now, though, my plan is to look through it all, pick a theme, and then think about what kind of special feature would work for it. They gave me a little bit of money to hire a freelancer to write something new, and I'd like to ask you once everything's decided."

I agreed immediately, delighted to help my friend with his first job.

He contacted me again about a month later…

Published in April 2006 in
a Certain Monthly Magazine

The Truth Behind the Mass-Hysteria Incident at the School Camping Trip

In 2002, an elite private middle school in Kansai called R became famous throughout Japan following news reports of a mass-hysteria incident that took place during a school camping trip. Extraordinary testimonies were gathered from multiple witnesses, but the most baffling were those from the students themselves.

Various media outlets obsessed over the mysterious happening, but it was eventually dismissed as a case of mass hysteria. Unsatisfied with this explanation, our team independently interviewed U, who was a second-year student at R Middle School at the time, to obtain a firsthand account of the events that unfolded that night. The full text follows.

******

The news said it was a case of mass hysteria, but it wasn't like that at all. Me and my friends all saw it, and so did our teachers.

It's been four years, but whenever I meet up with my classmates from back then, we never talk about it. It's like a taboo subject. I mean, someone died, after all.

Our school always holds an overnight camping trip for second-years. We do outdoor activities and the like. In previous years, kids went to Okayama, but we went to ●●●●●, to this sort of recreational facility. I think some company owns it. But you know all that—it was on the news.

The place had been built recently, so everything was in really good condition. I heard companies held training activities there when it wasn't being used for school events like ours. To be honest, we were all glad we didn't have to stay in some run-down youth retreat.

During the day, we did a short nature walk and cooked at a nearby campground. After sunset, we ate dinner in the dining hall, and then each class gave presentations and performances. It was pretty fun. Then, from around eight until lights-out, we had free time.

The building's main entrance faced the highway, but the bedrooms in the back looked out over the mountains.

There were four people to each room, and we all had a back door that opened onto a little balcony. Beyond the balcony was a dark forest leading up to the mountain. The building was two stories, and all the rooms had the same design, all facing the forest. During free time, some people hung out on their balconies and talked to the kids in the neighboring rooms. Some boys on the first floor were shouting to people on the second floor, playing the telephone game.

I was playing cards with my friends in our room when we heard a commotion out on the balconies. I was curious, so I asked the people outside what happened, and they said they'd heard a strange voice. We mumbled something like "Oh, sure. Real scary," and walked out to join them.

By then, everyone was cramming onto the balconies, and I heard the people above us say "What is it?" and "Did you hear that?" And sure enough, when I listened closely, I heard a voice coming from deep within the forest.

"Heeey."

It didn't sound like someone shouting for help. It was more like someone calling out to us. We could hear the voice over and over, at regular intervals. It sounded like a man.

There was a boy in another class who was known as a troublemaker, and he just had to shout back. He cried, "Hey! Hey!" and the voice called out again, saying, "Heeey." The boy kept responding and laughing with his friends.

They went back and forth like that until somebody said, "It's getting closer, isn't it?"

They were right. At first, the voice had been so faint that you could barely hear it. But now it was very clear. The only light was coming from our rooms, though, so we couldn't see more than a few meters into the forest. By then, the voice was loud enough that I think we could have seen the person if it had been daytime.

We all started to get nervous and scared. Some kids ran back into their rooms and closed the sliding door. Everyone was talking among themselves, and one of the other students said they would run and get a teacher.

Me? I was scared, of course, but I was too curious to run. Everyone in my room was on our balcony, looking out into the forest.

Then a girl on the balcony next to ours called out.

"Are you okay?"

She was in a different class, but she was their student representative and running for student council, so I knew who she was. Because of her character, I was pretty sure she wasn't joking around. She must have been genuinely concerned.

I remember that it suddenly went quiet as all the other kids waited for the voice to reply.

"Cooome! Come over heeere! I have persimmons!"

The words were very clear, but I'm not sure how to describe them. It was like the voice had no emotion to it. It came out in a flat monotone. It felt like whoever was speaking didn't understand the meaning of what they were saying. Like some animal was only mimicking a human's voice.

Everyone was more astonished than scared, but then the girl kept talking. I remember her voice was shaking slightly.

"What do you mean?"

Almost before she finished, the voice spoke again.

"Cooome! Come over heeere! I have persimmons! Cooome! Come over heeere! I have persimmons! Cooome! Come over heeere! I have persimmons! Cooome! Come over heeere! I have persimmons!"

It repeated the same words over and over.

Someone on another balcony screamed, and then everyone panicked and fled back into their rooms.

My group ran, too. We were practically crying. That's when we heard someone yell "Hey! Who are you?!" and realized it was a teacher. I couldn't see them from our room, but I could tell they were on one of the second-floor balconies. I was about halfway inside the room, looking back over my shoulder, when I saw a round light shining down on the forest. The teacher had a flashlight.

The light moved around the trees for a while until it briefly passed over something.

I'm still not sure what it was, but it looked like a person.

I didn't see the whole thing, just a pair of legs in the light. They were weirdly white, with enormous bare feet. Whoever it was wasn't wearing any shoes.

The feet were huge. Based on their size alone, I would've thought the person was three meters tall. But then they ran away and disappeared.

After that, the teachers gathered everybody together in the dining hall. They said they'd called the police about a trespasser and that we should stay inside that night and not go out on our balconies for any reason. Then they sent us back to our rooms. Lots of kids were in shock, and some even started feeling sick. We were supposed to go to the dam the next day, but the teachers canceled the tour, and we went home early.

The school later held a meeting to explain what had happened, and my mother attended. They said the police hadn't found any trace of a trespasser, and they warned everyone not to answer any questions from the media about the incident.

I don't think anyone outside my school knows about this next part, but after that incident, the girl who'd called out to the voice went a little crazy.

She'd stand up in the middle of class and shout, "I want to go to the mountain." Eventually, she stopped coming to school. And then, a few months later, she died. Our teachers never gave a clear explanation about what happened, but I heard rumors she killed herself. Someone in her class who went to the funeral said her casket was closed so you couldn't see her face.

They said they wished they could have seen her so they could say one last goodbye.

Published in August 1993 in
a Certain Monthly Magazine

Short Story: *Masshiro-san*

They say the children living in that apartment building lose their minds.

It was built six years ago in ●●●●●, during a wave of new construction, when they carved out half a mountain to make more room.

Though it was outside the city, the location was only a ten-minute drive away, and all the rooms were filled as soon as construction finished.

The multibuilding apartment complex contained over a thousand units and had its own park, making it feel like a small village. The new construction was a strange sight next to the old houses nearby, which were still inhabited by local residents.

Most of the apartments' tenants were families looking to raise their children away from the city, and soon the mothers had formed a little community, meeting up in the park with their young children and visiting neighbors for tea during the day.

A's family moved in as soon as the buildings went up.

There was A, who was a housewife; her husband; their ten-year-old daughter, B; and their cat. Each morning, her husband would head out to work and B would leave for school, while A would spend her day attending to housework and chatting with the other mothers outside, building their community.

Then, some months after their move, A realized something.

B had started acting strangely.

She'd always misbehaved now and then, just like any kid her age. But after they moved, things changed. She started behaving oddly, doing things like purposefully stepping on their cat's tail or squeezing tomatoes at the supermarket. A would scold B, and she'd nod along attentively, only to start up the behavior again later. A wasn't sure what to do about it.

She talked it over with her husband, and they decided to keep an eye on their daughter, figuring the cause was just stress from the new environment. Then one day, she casually mentioned her troubles to some of the other mothers. When she did, those with children near B's age started voicing the same complaints.

After moving to the apartment, the other children had also begun doing things they'd never done before—such as capturing butterflies and removing their wings before covering them in sand; dropping flowerpots from balconies; and kicking strollers with little babies in them.

At that, A remembered a recent incident where she'd scolded some elementary school–aged children who were ripping up flowers from the apartment's flower beds and tossing them on the ground.

The group of mothers began to suspect there was a problem at their children's new school. All the kids went to the same elementary school, after all, and they spent a lot of time there.

The school had been built long before to serve the local children. When the apartments were constructed, it was renovated and more teachers were hired to accommodate the influx of students. As a result, the student body was composed of both local children and kids from the apartment complex.

During a parent-visitation day, A and the other mothers asked one of the teachers if the students were engaged in any mischief or pranks at school. The teacher assured them nothing like that happened, then thought for a moment before telling them about a secret game that only the apartment kids played.

They wouldn't let local kids join in, and a few of them had come to the teacher crying about being excluded. It had caused some concern among the faculty.

That afternoon, A asked B about the game when she came home from school. B hesitated at first, but after swearing A to secrecy, she described it to her.

The game was called *Masshiro-san*, or Mister White.

B didn't know who started it. But every kid in the apartment complex played. Adults and local kids weren't allowed to join. It was a secret, just among the apartment kids. *Masshiro-san* was like tag. The game usually started with four to six people, but there was no set rule for the number of players.

First, the kids separated into boys and girls. The boys played rock-paper-scissors, and the loser became *Masshiro-san*. While the boys were doing that, the girls would run away. The boy representing *Masshiro-san* chased after the girls and tried to capture one. The other boys helped him by telling him where the girls were or by blocking them as they tried to get away. But only *Masshiro-san* was allowed to touch the girls.

When *Masshiro-san* managed to capture a girl, he would request a sacrifice.

The form of the sacrifice varied. It could be an eraser, or a pair of socks, or something else. But the girl had to give *Masshiro-san* something. She couldn't refuse, because otherwise something scary would happen.

The game ended when the captured girl handed over the sacrifice. It kept going until the sacrifice was handed over, even if it took hours or days. During that time, no one talked to the girl.

When she heard all this, A felt uneasy. It hardly sounded like a game children would play.

That evening, as her family slept, A heard the front door close. She and her husband slept in the same room, so it had to be B, who had gotten her own bedroom after the move.

A walked into the hall to find B taking off her shoes at the front door. She seemed to have just come back home.

A confronted her about what she had been doing out in the middle of the night, and B said that she had gone to hand over the sacrifice. When A asked who she had gone to see, B said only, "*Masshiro-san.*" A pressed her about the sacrifice, and B muttered, "Mike," the name of their cat.

In the living room, a flower vase lay near a small pool of blood, wet fur stuck to its surface.

A's family decided to move soon afterward.

Information from the Internet 1

Excerpt from *Forum for Sightings of Suspicious Persons*

Location: Close to the ●●●●● intersection
Time: October 19, 2018, around 4:20 PM
Description: Fifties, male, shaved head, chubby, on foot, wearing a blue jacket
Details: Approached elementary school girls on their way home and said he'd take them to the mountain.

Location: Near ●●●●● Elementary School
Time: May 27, 2020, around 11:30 AM
Description: Twenties, male, bleached hair, skinny, in a car, wearing a black hoodie
Details: Pointed his phone out of his car window at a woman walking down the street and asked her if she wanted to go to the mountain

Location: Near the ●●●●● highway
Time: June 3, 2021, around 9:00 PM
Description: Forties, male, short hair, medium build, on foot, wearing a suit
Details: Chased after a woman on a bicycle, yelling about wanting to go to the mountain with her

******

Excerpt from the August 19, 2016, Edition of XX Online Newspaper

On August 18, a resident living close to ●●●●● Dam called 9-1-1 to report something floating in the lake behind the dam. An officer from ●●●●● Station was dispatched, and they found a woman and a child floating in the water. The two were later confirmed dead.

According to ●●●●● Station, the bodies were identified as ○○○○ (35 years old) and her daughter, ○○○○ (12), both residents of Nagano City, Nagano. The police questioned the husband (35) about his involvement in the case.
The station received testimony from neighbors that the husband had been heard saying, "We're going to a mountain in ●●●●● soon to see someone who has looked after our family." But considering the significant distance from the suspect's house to ●●●●● Dam, the police are investigating the possibility he had an accomplice.

******

Excerpt from the live broadcast archives of *Yukihiro's Haunted Hot Spots*, dated May 27, 2020
*The video has been deleted, so the following was taken from a transcript posted on an online forum.

(Start of broadcast)

What's up, everyone? It's me, Yuki, the Haunting Hunter!

I've been receiving a lot of requests for this, and today, I'm finally making it out to ●●●●●.
My followers will already know about this place, but it's rumored to be one of the scariest paranormal hot spots in all of Kansai. It's particularly notable for just how many haunted locations there are around here. Dams, ruins, tunnels—it's practically a ghost department store. So how about we check them all out?! I'm going to start with ●●●●● Tunnel.

I see you all talking in the comments. Seems you want me to stop the chitchat and just head in. All right, here I go. Are you seeing this? I'm still in my car, but once I get out, I'll be standing at the tunnel's entrance. Ready?

(Sound of a door opening and closing)

As you can see, this place is totally deserted. It's three AM, so I guess that's to be expected. The tunnel is really huge. I better be careful not to get run over if a truck comes. So, according to a rumor on the internet, if you stand at the entrance where I am now— Oh, wait. There's an entrance on either side, isn't there? Anyway, they say a ghost will answer if you stand on the side where I

parked and call out toward the opening facing the dam. It's a really famous story.
We'll check out the tunnel later. Let's test this rumor first.

Oh, it got cold all of a sudden. What's that, chat? I don't need to sell it? Ha-ha. Okay, let's do this. Hellooo?

Nothing. I'll try again. Hellooo?

Yep, nothing. All right, let's head into the tun— Huh? What the hell?
I'm going back to the car.

(Sound of a door opening and closing)

Did you see it? You saw it, right? There was a figure walking toward me from the other side. Yeah. I couldn't really see because it was so dark. Maybe it was someone who lives around here.
What? You want me to go back out there? What if they call the police? I don't know. Well, I can see a lot of you are asking me to give it one more try.
Okay. I'll go talk to them and just pretend I got lost.

(Sound of a door opening and closing)

Excuse me. What the—? Ah!

(Sound of a door opening and closing, followed by an engine starting)

Whoa! What the hell was that? Damn. They had this big grin, and they were waving and running right toward me.

(Sound of a car moving)

That was really close. I'm freaked. You saw it, right? It was terrifying! If I'd started the car a second later, they would've reached me.
What the hell was that? A ghost? Are ghosts that corporeal?
First things first, I need to calm down. My heart is pounding.
I remember seeing a diner a ways back, so I'll keep driving until I reach it.

Seriously, what was that? If you guys hadn't told me to go back in, none of that would have happened. I'm kinda pissed. I can't believe you guys. Do you wanna die? What? What are all these comments about? Huh? No, I'm not acting weird. What's wrong? You guys are so irritating. Die, already. I'm way too terrified to head to the next location. But you all can't wait, right? I swear I'm gonna kill all of you. Today was just so… Ugh, die alrea…

(Five minutes of incoherent muttering)

Everyone, how about we go to the mountain?

(End of broadcast)

Letters to the Editor 1

Dear Editors of Monthly Magazine ○○○○,

My apologies for writing to you out of the blue.
My name is XXX, and I'm a university student living in Tottori.

I'm writing to ask for your help.
A strange man is following me.

I read your article on ●●●●● the other day, and I thought you might know something.
This letter will be a little long, but please read it all the way through and tell me what to do.

I think it was August of this year.
During summer break, me, my boyfriend, and one of our male friends went out for a drive. We decided to check out a paranormal hot spot, and we headed for ●●●●●. I mean, all the magazines mention it.

We were too scared to go at night, so we went there during the day.
That area has a lot of haunted locations like the apartment complex and that house, but enough people were around in the daytime that we weren't scared.
We went to Building Five—the one famous for suicides—then walked

around outside the haunted house and peeked in through the windows to see if we could spot any talismans. But nothing happened.

●●●●●, which is on the other side of the mountain, has a dam that's another hot spot for suicides, so we decided to drive over there, too.

It happened a little after we started down a narrow mountain road. My boyfriend was driving, and I was in the passenger seat.

A car came from the opposite direction. The road had two lanes, but there wasn't a lot of room, so we both slowed down to pass each other.

I was just staring blankly out the front window when I caught the man driving the other car staring at me, muttering something. I couldn't hear anything he said, of course, but I didn't like that he was looking at me and not at my boyfriend, who was driving.

We eventually reached the dam, but it was already dark, and we were too scared to get out and walk around.

So we drove a little farther down the highway to get a better view of the dam, then we went home.

It was already midnight by the time we got back to Tottori.

That was when it all started.

The next day, some other friends and I went out for drinks at a bar near our university.

There are a lot of restaurants and bars on that street, and at night, it gets pretty crowded with students and office workers on their way home from work.

Around nine o'clock, we decided to head to the next place, and we stood in front of the bar discussing where to go.

We were huddled together, talking, when one of my friends asked, "Who's that?"

She was pointing toward a narrow alley between two restaurants not too far from where we were standing.

Someone had poked their head out of the alley and was looking right at us, muttering something.

It was that man.

It really creeped me out. Some of my friends went over to check the alley, but they didn't find anyone there.

They told me it was probably just someone who looked similar, and I tried to convince myself they were right.

Then, a month or so later, I saw the man again.

It was evening, and I'd just gotten back to my apartment after finishing my classes for the day.

I was about to head inside, when I heard someone open the door to the next apartment over.

Figuring my neighbor was heading out, I paused to say hi to her. But what I saw instead was a man's face, staring at me.

It was him.

He seemed to be trying to say something to me, but I was so scared that I ran straight inside my apartment and locked the door.

I asked my friend to come over and spend the night.

My apartment is female-only, so my neighbor is a woman. She's lived alone ever since I moved in.

Naturally, I called the police, but my neighbor was in her apartment at the time with a friend, so they determined I had made a mistake.

Then, a couple of days later, it happened again.

* * *

I went to the bathroom between classes.
The toilets usually get crowded during breaks, but the ones in the research wing are rarely used, so I typically go there. At the time, all three stalls were empty.

I used the one farthest from the entrance.
After I finished, I noticed that the door of the stall next to mine was closed.
I hadn't heard anyone enter the bathroom, and a bad feeling came over me.

Just as I tried to sneak past it, the door creaked open, and a man's face peered out. He looked at me with a big grin and spoke.

"Please come again."

I ran past the stall, but I think that's what he said.
I'm not really sure, though, since I was screaming at the time.

After that, I didn't see him again in the real world.
Instead, I saw him in my dreams.

In the dream, I'm climbing a mountain at night.
There are lots of tall trees, and they block almost all the moonlight.
I'm climbing some old stairs carved into a mountain path.
There are stone lanterns to either side, but most of them have fallen over.
The stairs end at a crooked torii gate.

The man is waiting for me under the torii.
He stands there with that same grin, his big mouth opened wide.

The most disturbing thing for me is that, inside the dream, I'm not the slightest bit scared.
When I wake up, I feel calm.
Am I cursed?

Who is this man?

Please help.

**At the end of the letter is a handwritten note, probably made by an editor, that reads:*

"Received October 5, 2004. Addressed to the editors, but included no information regarding the sender, so we were unable to reach out for an interview. Publication pending."

About a Place in the Kinki Region 2

One month after our reunion at the *izakaya*, Ozawa sent me an e-mail.

I'd like to talk about that supplementary issue of ○○○○. *Can we meet? It's for work this time.*

I just happened to have an appointment scheduled near his workplace in Jinbocho a few days later, so we decided to get coffee at a café there.

We met in front of the café and headed inside. I went with black coffee, and he got a caffe latte. As soon as we'd placed our orders, he spread out a bunch of papers on the table. They were all copies of various articles.

As I read them, he watched with excited impatience.

The moment I finished, he started talking.

"To get straight to the point, I'd like you to write an article for the magazine. But first, let me tell you what I found."

Apparently, he'd continued to hole up in the company archives, checking through all the old materials related to the magazine.

But the shelves containing the scores of back issues were totally unorganized. Nothing was arranged by publication date, some issues were missing, and research materials and reader letters were all stuffed haphazardly into cardboard boxes. It was absolute chaos.

At first, he tried to read everything sequentially by publication year, but he abandoned that idea partway through and began simply reading whatever he happened to grab next. He'd planned to read all of it anyway, so there was no need to go through it in order. He could just take notes on the things that caught his attention and sort it all out later.

And as he combed through the heaps of materials, he discovered something.

Currently, Japan has over five hundred paranormal hot spots of various sizes, but only a few garner enough attention for a magazine or some other media outlet to run a story on it.

Among the most famous are Tama Cemetery and Ikoma Tunnel. Hokkaido and Okinawa have some places, too, but publishers prefer to minimize reporting costs, and that includes travel expenses. So they naturally tend to feature spots in Osaka, Tokyo, Fukuoka, and other big urban centers where there are freelance writers the editors know who are reasonably close to the sites in question.

Also, the more people visit a paranormal site, the more rumors about it start circulating. So places that are easy for thrill seekers and the curious to access receive the most notoriety.

Perhaps for that reason, though Ozawa was unfamiliar with such stories, by the time he'd read about ten issues of the magazine, he began to notice certain place names were coming up over and over.

"At first, I just thought, 'Oh wow, there it is again.' My parents took me camping around there when I was young. I think that's why it stood out to me."

He was talking about an area in the mountains of the Kinki region notorious for paranormal activity, centered around a tunnel, a dam, and a ruined building. The area was quite famous in certain circles, so I was well aware of it.

The three hot spots were all within a three-kilometer radius, and back during the paranormal craze, quite a few groups tried to hit all of them in a single night as a kind of test of courage. Thinking about it made me feel somewhat nostalgic.

However, all the stories associated with those places were just the typical fare. Things like, if you did so-and-so in the tunnel, a floating head would appear, or the ghosts of the people who killed themselves at the dam still haunted the grounds, or a woman's ghost wandered around in the basement of the ruined building. It was all standard stuff like that, as I recalled. In recent years, the area had gained a solid reputation among thrill seekers as being one of the top paranormal hot spots in the country, but no one in the media wrote about it anymore. It was already old hat.

Even Ozawa, who was quite a bit younger than me, had begun to get the same impression. He kept encountering similar stories to those of other famous haunted spots and was getting a little fed up.

"After reading some more articles, though, I began to wonder if the stories from those three spots were all related, if they could have come from the same root cause."

Then he pointed to the papers in my hands.

"*A True Story! New Developments Regarding a Missing Girl in Nara?*, *The Truth Behind the Mass-Hysteria Incident at the School Camping Trip*, and *A Peculiar Comment* were all written in different decades. Yet the same name kept popping up in all of them, and that caught my eye. That's right, I'm talking about the same area around ●●●●● I just mentioned. But none of these stories are associated with any of those paranormal hot spots. They just happened to all occur in ●●●●●. The ruin was still a regular building at the time those students had their camping trip, so I doubt it was considered a paranormal hot spot back then. Even so, all three stories take place in ●●●●●, and the word 'mountain' plays a pivotal role in each one. Don't you find that strange?"

All the other stories associated with this area's three hot spots were run-of-the mill urban legends, with no obvious connection, so the odd link between these three involving the mountain had stood out to Ozawa.

"Once I noticed it, I couldn't get it out of my head. So I put aside the old magazines for a moment and started searching the internet. First, I checked an online map to see if the torii in *A Peculiar Comment* actually existed. And sure enough, the street view showed a ruined torii and a set of stairs leading to the top of the mountain on the east side of the dam's lake. From that, I assumed the 'mountain' mentioned in the stories was the one to the east of the area that had the dam, ruins, and tunnel. Next, I searched the internet for any similar stories related to a mountain in ●●●●●, and this is what I found."

With that, he handed me some printouts of online articles and forum posts. He had searched combinations of the keywords ●●●●●, *mountain*, *creepy story*, *ghost*, and *incident*. The results of those searches surprised me.

"There's a YouTuber's live stream that went wrong, reports on suspicious people that have nothing to do with any urban legends or ghost stories, even an article discussing a suspected murder. And all of them are somehow related to this 'mountain.'"

Considering all the evidence, I had a hard time dismissing it as mere coincidence. Then, after I'd sat for a moment in stunned silence, he presented me with two more documents: a letter in an envelope and a copy of an article from one of the magazine's back issues. He waited for me to read them before continuing.

"I'd been digging through research materials and notes at the same time as the back issues. At first, I was just browsing, but once I noticed the relationship between the mountain and ●●●●●, I decided to reread them. This letter doesn't mention the mountain directly, but it's in there. What caught my attention was that the woman who wrote it first visited some haunted sites, then crossed over a mountain to get to a dam. If we put the mountain at the center, the three hot spots I mentioned earlier are to the west. The mountain belongs to a range running from north to south, so we can eliminate those sides. That means the woman visited additional sites to the east of the mountain, implying there are various other paranormal hot spots scattered around it, aside from the dam, ruin, and tunnel. And what do you know? Two of the notes about suspicious people are from the east side of the mountain, and so is the story about *Masshiro-san*. The complex is currently called the ghost apartments."

He showed me all this on an online map as he spoke, running his finger over the pins he'd dropped on each paranormal hot spot and tracing a circle around the mountain.

I had heard about some of the sites to the east.

They included a ruined house and an abandoned apartment complex located near the foot of the mountain that the locals said were haunted. But the three spots to the west were more well known, and only magazines geared toward real aficionados, like the old monthly version of ○○○○, ever mentioned the sites to the east.

In addition, because the mountain lay on the border of two prefectures, no one ever linked the three western spots in one to the two eastern spots in the other, to form one large area of paranormal activity. But according to Ozawa's explanation, it was more natural to think of all five sites as a single region surrounding the mountain.

I explained this, and Ozawa nodded.

"I guess ghosts and specters don't care about arbitrary human boundaries… But now I'm sure of it. The central theme of this supplementary issue will be investigating whether the paranormal activity in this region is linked to the mountain. I'll pull related stories from back issues and the boxes of research materials to fill it out. It would make me really happy as a new editor if I could bring the readers a fresh insight they've never heard before."

Listening to Ozawa's idea, I was impressed with the passion he brought to his work. But at the same time, I thought he sounded a little overzealous.

"And that, at last, brings me to the topic at hand. I want you to write a story about this region. You can use any style you want, and there's no word limit. However, I have a few additional requests. I'd like you to review whatever materials I find and study them with me. Please also share any similar stories you've worked on in the past and ask around to see if any of your contacts have more information. I'd like you to write something new based on our findings."

The compensation he quoted me wasn't enough to justify the work involved. But swayed by his passion and my own curiosity as a horror fan, I decided to take the job.

"I'll keep digging through the archives. Right now, we have far fewer articles about the east side, so I'll try to find anything I can about those sites, regardless of the subject. Right now, we only have *Masshiro-san*, and that doesn't have anything to do with the mountain… Hopefully I'll find other stories with some kind of connection, and those will give us something to consider. I'll also keep an eye out for any stories about the area around the mountain or the shrine there."

This is how I came to investigate ●●●●●. As my first step, I decided to reach out to a certain person…

Published in August 2009
in a Certain Monthly Magazine

Readers Column

Instead of the Eight-Foot-Tall Woman, my hometown has the Jumping Lady.

She's a woman with a huge smile who jumps really high to look inside houses, up to the windows on the second floor or to the sliding doors on apartment balconies.

She only does it to houses with kids, though, and it happened to one of my classmates.

Please investigate!

(Maa-chan, fourteen years old, ●●●●●)

Published in February 2015
in a Certain Monthly Magazine

Short Story:
A House to Rent

This story is about A, a freelance designer living in Kokura, Fukuoka.

"I was born and raised in Tokyo, so I've always wanted to live in a smaller city. A large part of why I became a freelancer was so I could work from anywhere."

Spurred on by the recent wave of de-urbanization, A left her job at a major advertising agency six months ago and began her new career.

"Well before I quit, I had been looking online for places to live. Recently, local governments have been helping renovate vacant houses into affordable rentals for single people moving into the area. Lots of them are quite stylish, and I used to spend every night checking listings and imagining living there. It was kind of like my hobby."

At the time, A was considering moving somewhere other than Kokura.

"I was looking at an area called ●●●●●, in the Kinki region. Some vacant houses in a historical residential area had been turned into rental properties."

A didn't want to move to some tiny, remote village where all her neighbors would be hundreds of meters away. She just wanted to escape the bustle of Tokyo and to breathe some fresh air. This area seemed ideal for her purposes.

Heart set on the location, she began researching rental properties.

"I usually do an internet search with the location name, plus 'renovation,' 'rent,' and 'house.' That brings up pictures of the interiors, exteriors, and floor plans all in one place, so I don't have to keep clicking through info on a property just to get a good look at it. Instead, I can see everything at once, then click on the pictures that look interesting to find out more."

One evening after work, A was sitting in bed searching through renovated properties in the ●●●●● region.

"I don't remember exactly what keywords I used, but I think they were something like 'rent' and '●●●●●.'"

Starting at the top of the list, she checked exterior photos, floor plans, and so on, until she noticed a strange image on her screen.

"The picture in the search results was small, so I clicked on it and opened the source web page to get a better look."

The picture showed a woman standing in the dark.

"The lighting in the image was really bad, and I couldn't make out that much. But it was this eerie picture of a woman in a red coat with long, ruffled hair. She was standing stiffly upright in a run-down Japanese style room."

Above the picture was a line of garbled text, but nothing else, no links to other pages. The site seemed to exist solely to host this picture.

"It was nighttime, and it spooked me a little, but I brushed it off and went back to the image-results page to continue checking listings."

She kept scrolling, until something caught her eye about ten minutes later.

"At first, I thought it was the same image. But something about it felt different."

The next thing she knew, she'd opened the image.

"It looked like the photo was taken in the same run-down Japanese style room. It was the same woman, too. But this time, her arms were raised."

Once again, there was a line of garbled text over the image, but it looked slightly longer than before.

"The fact it was longer meant there must have been something different written there before the text got corrupted. Whoever uploaded those images was trying to say something to the person on the other side of the screen, and that really creeped me out."

Unnerved, A stopped looking at listings for the night. From the following day on, she used the image-search function a lot less.

"I'm not sure how long it was after that. I had almost forgotten about the whole thing, so it must have been around a month or so. My boss asked me to copy some documents for an upcoming meeting."

As she waited for the copier to finish printing, A leaned against the machine, staring blankly at the stream of repeating pages flowing out. Suddenly, something strange caught her eye. She quickly paused the job and riffled through the stack of papers to find what had grabbed her attention.

"The copies were black and white, so the image was in gray scale, but it was a picture of that woman. The copier had printed a picture of the woman with the raised hands standing in that room. The image didn't fill the whole sheet of paper, though. There was a little space above that had some blocky, handwritten text."

"Thank you for finding me."

A panicked briefly, then she crumpled the paper into a ball, stuffed it in her pocket, and finished her day.

After work, A called a friend from elementary school and invited her over.

"I was scared to be alone and knew I had to do something about that paper, but I didn't know what."

She explained everything that had happened, then watched, terrified, as her friend smoothed out the crumpled sheet of paper. She saw the same eerie woman in the image, just as she had back at work. But now that she looked again, something about the background felt off to her.

While A turned away, her friend froze, eyes locked on the paper. She sat silently like that, until A asked what was bothering her. Then she spoke, her voice shaky.

"Isn't this your parents' house?"

"It was my bedroom at my parents' house. My friend recognized it because she used to come over when we were in school together. I could tell it was my room based on the shape of my desk and the unique clock on the wall. The moment she said it, I knew she was right."

A found her current house in Kokura through a real estate agent's website, not an image search.

Information from the Internet 2

Excerpt from an internet forum called *Stories That Will Give You Goose Bumps*, found on an aggregator website

Name: Anonymous-But-True Horror Stories
Date Posted: 05/17/10 (Mon) 20:30:43
ID: ZDKsJPWc0

I'm posting because the stuff about that creepy blog reminded me of this story. I don't post stuff on the internet much, so sorry for any mistakes.
This happened about five years ago, but I still wonder about that blogger.

I've loved motorcycles since I was in my twenties, and I used to go searching for blogs by other bikers like me.
I don't remember how I found this particular one, but the guy rode the same model of Suzuki as I did, so I probably found it while searching for stuff about that bike. I think it was on FC2, and it seemed like just some middle-aged man's hobby blog. It didn't have many likes or comments, and I could tell it was purely for this guy's personal satisfaction. The site contained a lot of posts, though. I think he'd been using it for a while as a kind of journal. He covered a lot of helpful topics such as how to do custom work and maintenance, so I checked the blog often, but I never left any comments.
The blog was about half what I just described and half trip reports with pictures. The reports didn't talk about anything special. It was just stuff like pictures of his bike at Lake Biwa and comments about how much he loved the soft serve at some random roadside station.

Then things took a weird turn. One day I opened the blog from my bookmarks bar, just like I always did, and found he'd deleted all his previous posts. He'd been posting as usual only three days before.
All the info in the profile section had disappeared, and his profile photo, which used to be a picture of his bike, was now a black square.

It was like everything on the blog had vanished overnight.
The blog was so empty that, for a second, I thought I'd accidentally gone to the wrong site. But the title was still there, and it was definitely that guy's blog.

His list of posts now had only one entry.
It was new, and the title was just one letter: "A."
His titles were usually descriptive, like "Trip to Kochi on X Month, X Day" or "How to Maintain Your Tires," so this slapdash label was really unusual.
Something else was weird, too. The post was locked.
It required a password to access it.

Though we'd never met, as a frequent reader, I felt a kind of connection with this guy, so I really wanted to know what was in the post. I thought it might even explain why he'd erased his blog.
I searched the site for a password but couldn't find anything. Well, everything had been deleted, so there weren't many places to look.
Eventually, I gave up and started trying random passwords. Things like the name of the blog, the bike he rode, 0000, and so on. But nothing worked.
I chose four numbers and decided to give it one last go.
It was his birthday. I knew the date because it was the same as mine.
I remembered seeing it on his profile when I first started reading his blog.
To my surprise, the numbers worked. I still remember feeling kind of giddy.

The post titled "A" didn't have any words, just pictures.
The first one looked like a roadside station. His bike was there, so I assumed he'd taken the photo himself.
Up until then, I'd thought that maybe someone hacked his blog. But this was proof he was the one who made the post.
I think the second picture was of a dam. It was a picture of his bike next to a sign reading ●●●●● Dam, with a lake visible in the background.
I assumed these were pictures he'd taken for a trip report.

The next one showed a ruined torii gate at the base of a mountain with stairs leading up the slope. That was when the pictures started getting weird. I think he was taking photos as he climbed the stairs, because there were pictures of the sky above, of the surrounding forest, and of the top of the stairs. It felt like he was taking photos at random, rather than trying to capture any specific images.
After that came a picture of the main shrine, but it was cut off and only partly in frame. The image was out of focus and blurry, so it was hard to make out,

but the building looked to be in disrepair, with a collapsed roof. The doors were closed, so I couldn't see inside.

The next photo showed a little shrine called a *hokora*, like the kind you sometimes see by the side of the road. It was about as tall as the guy, with double doors under a small roof. The composition of the photo was strange, like he'd clicked the button at random with the camera tilted. The *hokora* was a lot smaller than the main shrine, but it looked just as run down, and its doors were also closed.

The next picture showed the same *hokora*. But this time, its doors were open. *Hokora* are usually meant to enshrine some sacred item. But this one had a bunch of dolls crammed inside. Barbie dolls, fancy porcelain dolls, traditional Japanese dolls, anime figures, dolls of all types, sizes, and eras filled the little structure, right up to the ceiling.

The next photo was the last one.

It showed a man's back as he bowed toward the *hokora*.

That was where the post ended.

After I finished looking at the post, I went back to the main page and saw a new entry in the list; it hadn't been there before.

This post was titled "It's All Over."

The new post was also locked, but I couldn't figure out the password.

About a month or so later, the whole blog disappeared.

This is just my assumption, but I think the man in the last picture was the guy who owned the blog. He was dressed like a biker, after all.

But in that case, who took the photo?

I hope that guy is okay.

Transcript of an Interview 1

Wow, it's been ages. We haven't seen each other since that horror talk show in Shibuya. That's almost ten years, right?

What do you want to order? Yeah, I'll have an iced coffee, black. What, you want the same thing? Ha-ha. I remember when we always had iced coffees at meetings and joked about how easy we were to order for.

Yeah, I'm freelancing. Fortunately, my connections from when I was an editor have kept me in business. I'm not working on anything paranormal anymore, though. I mean, there's not much money there. I'm not into horror like you are. They just happened to assign me to that department.

But it's nice to hear from someone I used to work with.

Don't be so formal. I'm not a client anymore. If anything, you have more experience in this genre than I do.

After that? It was a mess. Management suddenly

told us we had to stop printing. Well, there had been rumors it might happen. The magazine wasn't selling well after the chief editor changed, and by the end, the whole department had shrunk to just three people. I'm sorry for calling you so suddenly with the bad news back then. And right when you were working on a piece for us…

The three of us quit when they dissolved the editorial department. I doubt any of the other departments would have wanted someone from a discontinued publication. I'd already been considering freelancing anyway. The other editor, O, found a job at a different publisher soon after he quit. I still see him. He sometimes has odd jobs for me. You never met him or the other editor, did you?

The chief editor? Oh, you mean S. I wonder what he's doing now. I have no idea. We weren't close. S quit first and never said anything to the rest of us.

I can say this now, but I never liked him. Why? Well, it comes down to editorial philosophy, but O and I wanted to make ○○○○ more like an entertainment magazine, while S was more focused on factual reporting.

The element of reality is what makes paranormal stuff fun, of course. Readers want real stories, not fiction. But when it comes down to it, what they really want is entertainment. I think it's okay to embellish real events, so long as the readers enjoy them.

But S wasn't like that. He wanted evidence or reliable sources for every project or draft. But how can you get evidence when you're dealing with ghosts and aliens, right? We can't know if our informants' stories are real, and there's not enough time to do detailed interviews for each story. It wasn't like we were writing for a newspaper. But S wouldn't accept anything that couldn't be proved. I don't know how many times we argued over it.

But we were adults and S was the chief, so in the end, we did what he wanted. But there were a bunch of times when O and I secretly disagreed with him. That's one of the reasons we were so happy to have you around. You always delivered such high-quality work. All three of us trusted you. That, at least, we agreed on. We rarely ever had to ask you to redo a story.

You're kind of a rarity in this industry, you know.

I learned a lot from you about perspective and story structure.

Come to think of it, there's actually one more thing I can't forgive S for. I just said that the department dissolved and everyone quit, but I asked someone working in HR at the time, and they told me a different story.

Apparently, the whole thing started because S declared one day that he was going to resign. When upper management heard that, they suspended the magazine. I don't know how much of that is true, but if it is, then it would make a lot more sense that they suddenly stopped publication right in the middle of the fiscal year.

Well, whatever. If he wanted to quit, that's his business. But I wish he'd explained the situation to O and me. Just sending all your work to the remaining employees on your last day and saying good-bye is unacceptable. Anyway, ○○○○ was suspended, so there wasn't really anything to hand off or take over for any of us.

What? The archive is a mess? Ha-ha. Sorry about that. That's our fault. I feel bad for whoever had to come in after us. But it's good to hear that the magazine is still going, even if it's just irregular supplementary issues.

Sorry. I got all nostalgic and started babbling. We're talking about ●●●●● today, right?

Hey, I see you're using a tape recorder. Yeah, I know it's an app on your phone, but I still say "tape recorder" out of habit. Ha-ha.

I'm usually the one asking the questions, so I feel a little weird being interviewed. Have you been recording this whole time? Hey, no fair. Please keep that first part about the editorial department off the record.

Yeah, I remember. I went out there once for a report. I can't recall what I was there for… Oh yeah, that's right. There was a tunnel. We spent all night investigating a paranormal phenomenon.

But nothing happened, so we just published a picture with a hazy orb and ran that.

Magazines on the paranormal were pretty popular at the time. I actually enjoyed the job quite a bit. One of the guys who worked on the magazine before me said he wrote an article on a religious facility around that area. It was a different time back then, huh?

What you told me over the phone surprised me. That newbie you mentioned is pretty sharp. I never realized that mountain was such a paranormal hot spot. But now that you point it out, I think you're right.

Like I said before, it's embarrassing to admit, but after the higher-ups decided to stop publication, everybody was just focused on what they'd do next. All we did before leaving was stuff the back issues, data, and other paper documents into boxes, then cram everything into the archive.

When we left, our files, project data from freelancers, and research notes were still on our computers. We never transferred them back to the company to hold on to. I bet O did the same. I still have it all. When you contacted me, I went back through it for the first time in ages.

I just glanced through everything, but I found a story on ●●●●● that was never published. Something from—as your newbie would say—the east side of the mountain, the other side from the dam.

Unfortunately, the story never made it to the

draft stage, so I'll have to relate it based on my notes and what I remember.

******

The informant was XXXXXX, but I'll call him A. According to my notes, he was a twenty-two-year-old college student. F, a freelancer, introduced me to him.

I interviewed him on March 4, 2012.

A was studying psychology at a university in Tokyo. The Tohoku earthquake had just happened the year before, which made finding a job very difficult for him. Still, he'd managed to land something that started in April and he'd already submitted his graduation thesis, so he was relieved and excited for the future.

The story was about his thesis.

The title of his research was "Body Language When Displaying Fear and Similar Emotions to Others."

In the study, he showed people a short, scary video and then noted what physical gestures test subjects made when they related their experience to another person.

The study was quite unique. Apparently, A was a big horror fan and thought he'd have more fun doing a research project involving something he liked.

* * *

He wasn't just interested in what gestures were most common, though. He also wanted to study how his test subjects' personalities influenced the results. So A separated the subjects into groups.

To do this, he gave them a survey with ten or so questions that covered a wide range of descriptors, like "I like horror / I don't like horror," "I like talking / I don't like talking," or "I have siblings / I don't have siblings." A took the responses and body language data from about fifty subjects, and he tried to determine if any of the opposing groups showed a significant difference.

Because his study focused on body language when conveying fear, A wanted to avoid showing the participants a movie where the fear came from the story itself. He wanted something abstract that would give the person watching it a pure sense of terror. In the end, he chose a "cursed video" submitted to an online video-hosting site.

I'm sure you're familiar with the movie *The Ring*. In that film, anyone who watches a certain cursed video is supposed to die seven days later. The eerie but completely nonsensical cursed video featured in the movie became a social phenomenon. As you probably remember, video-hosting sites were flooded with self-made "cursed videos" in the wake of the movie's popularity.

The video A chose didn't really stand out in any way. It ran for about three minutes, changing images every few seconds. The pictures were of stereotypical stuff like blood-covered knives, a pixelated human figure in an abandoned building, or a woman with a frightening face.

When A saw the video, he recognized some of the images as scenes from famous horror movies. In other words, it was a low-quality amateur creation made by splicing together scary clips. The video? I tried to find it for our interview today, but I guess it's already been deleted. I couldn't manage to track it down.

A showed the video to his subjects, then he asked them to describe their feelings after watching it. He received a variety of answers. One person hugged themselves and said they were scared, while another said it reminded them of a nightmare they used to have. However, because of the topic he'd chosen, A had a hard time finding fifty people for his study.

To sidetrack for just a second, it's a pretty interesting experiment, right? When I was interviewing him, I got so sucked in that I totally forgot I was there reporting on a scary story. The results? Yeah, of course I asked him about that.

He categorized each body movement by "type," "frequency," and "duration." Most of the questions didn't result in any significant differences, but he saw a clear distinction between people who liked horror and those who didn't.

Specifically, those who liked horror would spend more time imitating the movement and appearance of ghosts than those who didn't. You know, they would hold their hands out in front of them and moan. Things like that.

In contrast, people who disliked horror would use filler gestures more frequently and for longer durations. By filler gestures, he meant meaningless actions like moving your hands while talking. You know, like the filler words people insert in sentences.

A analyzed this tendency so he could include it in his thesis.

He found that people who like horror still feel scared, but they enjoy that experience and want others to feel the same fear and joy. So they recreate details to convey the essence of the ghost or other scary experience in an effort to entertain the listener by scaring them.

People who dislike horror, however, view being scared as an unpleasant experience and want their listener to feel empathy and compassion for them. Their emotions tend to outpace their speech, resulting in more frequent filler gestures.

I found the whole thing so illuminating. Yeah, I was fascinated. In a way, it reminded me of the relationship between the publishers of paranormal magazines and their readers.

We provide our readers with the paranormal content they crave, doing everything we can to make it entertaining. But some of those readers experience strong reactions to certain information.

They're the people who get worked up enough to contact the editor. You brought it up earlier. Yeah, I'm talking about the letters from the readers.

We received a lot more for the issues that talked about ●●●●●. Not stuff like "I saw a UFO," but things like "I'm scared, and I need help."

Oops, I got really off topic there. Sorry, I've always been a blabbermouth.

Anyway, during his research, A analyzed the gestures of fifty people. All by hand, all by himself. I was surprised he'd taken such an analog approach.

First, he recorded his subjects describing their experience to someone else. Then he reviewed the tapes and noted in an Excel spreadsheet all the gestures each subject made, including the type, frequency, and duration of each gesture and the subject's profile. Finally, he tallied the results. The scary video was only three minutes long, but his subjects talked for about five minutes. Some even kept going for over ten minutes. It took A quite a lot of time and effort.

But once he'd finished recording the data for about twenty subjects, he started to get the hang of it. He began to enjoy himself and would try to guess in advance how each subject would act.

In the end, two of the subjects' actions stood out.

One was male—the other was female. Their gestures

weren't particularly notable, but while talking, both of them would sometimes turn their gaze away from the listener, almost like they had noticed something in another part of the room.

They both looked at the same spot, diagonally in front of them and to the right, just outside the camera's frame. But as far as A could remember, there was nothing there. It was just an empty corner of the room.

Neither seemed to be purposefully turning toward the corner; the action appeared almost subconscious. Sometimes they stopped what they were saying and stared at the spot. It almost seemed to A like they were responding to someone calling their name.

But A had intentionally removed anything that would make noise or otherwise interrupt the data-collection process. So he found their actions very strange.

If it had been only one person, he might have dismissed it as an individual quirk. But if two people were repeatedly gazing in the same exact direction, there might be some discernible cause. With that in mind, he decided to review their questionnaires.

I actually failed to mention something earlier. When A made the questionnaire, he added one item just for fun. It was "I have a sixth sense / I don't have a sixth sense."

So, as you've probably guessed, out of all fifty people, those two were the only ones to claim they had a sixth sense.

As I mentioned, A had a strong interest in horror and the supernatural, and this piqued his interest. So he asked both of them back individually to follow up. At first, neither wanted to talk about it, but A persisted until they agreed.

For the most part, their stories matched. Both said they had heard a persistent sound as they spoke.

It came from the corner of the room, continuing irregularly, with no discernible source. *Thump, thump.*

They both immediately realized it was a paranormal phenomenon. They'd lived their whole lives hearing and seeing things others couldn't, and the noise was just another encounter for them, so they didn't say anything about it.

But both of them unconsciously reacted to the noise, and A had noticed.

He asked if either of them believed the room was haunted, and they both gave the same answer.

They assumed the specter came not from the room but from the video in the experiment, because the noise would stop when they weren't talking about the movie.

In addition to the sound, the man reported seeing a black figure.

It moved up and down in the corner of the room in

time with the noise, almost like each *thump* came from the echo of the figure jumping.

The man added, "It's usually best to ignore them. They tend to cause trouble once they realize you can see them. I wouldn't probe any further if I were you."

Hearing a warning from someone who knew about ghosts scared A, and he stopped his inquiry after that. He never watched the video again, either.

But a line had already been crossed.

About a month later, A was in the thick of his graduation research. He was spending every day on campus, working on his thesis late into the night. He lived alone in an apartment two train stations away from the university, so he was staying with a friend who lived closer to campus.

Then one day, he got a phone call from an unknown number. It was the police.

The night before, a neighbor had called them to report a woman on A's balcony.

The caller lived in a house across from his apartment building, and they could see his balcony from their living room window.

Around nine pm, they looked toward the apartment and saw a woman in a reddish coat standing with both arms in the air on the balcony of a corner unit on the fifth floor—A's room.

She was facing A's apartment and periodically jumping up and down.

The caller assumed she was arguing with her boyfriend and he'd locked her out on the balcony, so they didn't pay much attention to it and went to bed. But when they woke up around three in the morning to use the bathroom and glanced toward the balcony, she was still there, facing A's apartment and periodically jumping. Astonished, the caller stared for a while, transfixed. That was when they realized there was something strange about the woman.

Her neck would tilt wildly every time she jumped. When she landed, the impact would fling her head around as though she were a baby with undeveloped neck muscles.

By the time the police arrived, she had disappeared, and no one answered when they knocked on A's door. The next morning, they asked the apartment manager for the resident's number and called him.

A couple of days later, A got another call, this time from his apartment's management office. His downstairs neighbor had filed a complaint.

The neighbor said they'd recently started hearing a thudding sound from the ceiling every day after midnight and they wanted him to keep it down. Since the police had already been called a few days before, the office issued him a warning and even threatened to evict him.

A rarely went home after that. Who would, after finding out a ghost had invaded their apartment?

He got a few more noise complaints from the management office, but he told them he spent almost no time at home, and they eventually stopped calling.

He was terrified the woman would follow him when he moved for his new job in April, so he asked for help from a writer he knew who happened to specialize in this kind of thing. That was F, who introduced me to him. F asked me for advice, and I arranged to interview A in exchange for information about a temple capable of exorcising the evil spirit.

******

What do you think? Heh-heh. Not satisfied, are you? Didn't think so. You're right, I never brought up ●●●●●.

But there's more. I'm sure you're curious about the cursed video. Yes. I immediately looked it up.

A said he just picked something at random for his study, so I suspect he didn't know that the video he chose is actually somewhat famous. Well, maybe famous is the wrong word. But it's discussed a lot on internet forums and the like.

One thread I found linked the video and insisted that watching it would actually curse you. A few people claimed it had made them feel sick or caused problems in their lives related to the supernatural.

Then, as you might expect, various internet sleuths started identifying the clips. One part came from some American film. Another was a supposedly haunted GIF that made the rounds a few years back. It's amazing how good people are at that kind of thing.

But there was one part no one could identify. It didn't seem to have come from any existing footage. Specifically, it was one scene with two parts. Together, it was about five seconds long and shot in black and white. Everyone thought it was some amateur recording.

I watched it, too. The scene in question didn't have the impact of the other parts, but it stood out for being particularly incomprehensible.

It starts with a building with the number five on it. You know how they number apartment buildings? It was like that. The shot of the building was taken from the ground.

Then the video cut to a close-up of a woman's face. She looked like she was smiling, or crying, or maybe angry. Her mouth was open in a wide grin that showed all her teeth. Her face got closer to the camera, then backed away. The sudden shot of her face was startling, and she only appeared for a few seconds, so it was difficult to tell, but I think she was jumping up toward the camera. It was like someone was standing above her, recording her as she looked up and jumped in their direction. Both her hands were extended above her head, as though she was reaching for the camera.

Exactly. The woman in A's story did the same

thing. But A didn't see her, so we can't be sure it was the same person.

Understandably, the same internet sleuths tried to identify that part of the cursed video as well. The building in the first shot was determined to be Building Five of the ghost apartments in ●●●●●. Based on the exterior and the mountain ridge visible in the background, it's almost certain.

But no one could identify the woman. The video only showed her face and hands, after all. The only other thing they were able to determine was that the ground beneath her was covered in gravel. The people in the thread picked the whole thing apart, but no one ever figured out who she was or where the video had been recorded.

The ghost apartments have a lot of creepy stories attached to them, so the people in the thread concluded it was this clip that caused the curse.

And that's where the story ends.

Why didn't we publish it, you ask? Oh, well. That's because the chief editor shelved it. He said the ending wasn't strong enough. In other words, we didn't get close enough to the truth. That's just how he was.

I actually agree with him. The story feels incomplete. It's messy. We'd need more evidence if we wanted to bill it as an investigation into the truth of the matter, and there isn't enough there for readers to have fun making up their own theories, either. It's too bad, really.

* * *

The story was scrapped, so you can write about it if you'd like. I'm sure you could do something with it. Then it can finally be put to bed. No, really. Go for it. You've done so much for us. I enjoyed talking with you. It really brings me back.

I'll ask O for any unpublished info about ●●●●●, too. I haven't talked with him in a while, so it'll be a good opportunity to reach out.

Published in March 2014
in a Certain Monthly Magazine

Short Story: *Waiting*

"I found the place kind of depressing."

A's father passed away from an illness shortly before his seventieth birthday, leaving his septuagenarian wife a widow.

A, who was forty at the time, was the couple's only son. He'd left home and moved to another city some time ago and now worried about his mother living on her own.

"She seemed so lonely, all by herself in that house…"

Then one day, his mother called and told him she was moving into an apartment.

She would rather move somewhere new than stay in the house by herself. In an apartment, she and her neighbors could look out for one another.

A real estate agent helped her find a place in ●●●●●. It was built on land carved out from the side of a mountain, and the pictures online showed exquisite views. It seemed like a nice place for her to spend the rest of her days.

But when A toured the complex with his mother and the real estate agent, he began to change his mind. The first line of this article describes his thoughts at the time.

"There weren't many people. It felt empty. The buildings themselves were large, and the complex had lots of them, but it seemed like only twenty percent of the rooms were occupied. I swear most of the windows didn't have curtains."

A didn't like the place. It seemed deserted to him, but his mother appreciated the peace and quiet.

At the agent's recommendation, A and his mother viewed a room on the third floor of Building Five, and they wound up signing a lease right then and there.

A's work started getting busy just as his mother began the next chapter of her life in the new apartment, so he wasn't able to visit her again until about six months later.

"The place still felt depressing. But my mom appeared to be doing fine, which was a relief. She said she'd even made some friends."

Something about her seemed a little off, however.

"She kept staring blankly out the window whenever we weren't talking. She didn't really do anything else. I started to wonder if she might be developing dementia."

Worried, A asked his mother what she was looking at; her answer was very brief.

"I'm waiting."

She didn't say any more.

That night, they heard a loud noise outside the window, interrupting their dinner. There was a thud and a crash at about the same time.

Surprised, A ran to the window. His mother, however, moved with unusual speed and beat him there.

Down below, he saw the body of a person twitching in a pool of blood, their arms and legs bent at odd angles.

After taking in the shocking sight, A turned toward his mother, and a wave of terror came over him.

She was staring down at the scene below, smiling.

After that, A sent her to live with some relatives until he could arrange for her to settle in with him. As he watched the moving truck take her things from the apartment and set off toward his house, a middle-aged woman called out to him from the park attached to the complex.

She introduced herself as someone from another building who knew his mother.

A informed her that his mother was moving and thanked her for looking out for her.

The woman replied, "I'll miss her, but I think it's for the best. She shouldn't stay in a place like that…"

Apparently, it wasn't the first time someone had committed suicide there. It turned out that a number of people jumped off the roof of Building Five every year. Among certain circles, it was quite notorious.

The jumpers weren't people living in the apartment complex, either. Most of them came from far away just to end their lives. For some reason, it only happened at Building Five, so the other residents tended to keep their distance.

A was shocked to find out his mother had been living in such a place.

Just then, something occurred to A, and he asked if there had been any other suicides since his mother had moved in.

Apparently, two people had already jumped to their deaths.

When he heard that, A was convinced.

His mother had been waiting for someone to jump.

Rough Draft of *Waiting*

The draft has a sticky note attached to the first page with the following memo written in red ink:

"With the new layout, this article has been reduced from four pages to two. Please cut out some of the details and rework it into a scary story focusing on the jumpers!"

******

A's mother was a gentle woman who was always smiling.

A had lived with his parents in Okayama until he was about twenty years old.

He moved out when he got a job in Nagano. Two decades later, his father suffered a stroke. Help arrived too late, and he passed away at the hospital later that same day.

A worried about his mother and suggested that she move in with him. But she didn't want to burden her only son, so she refused. A was in his forties and still single; his mother was probably worried she'd make it even harder for him to find a wife.

He went back to check on her whenever he could, each time noting how lonely she looked living all by herself in that big house at seventy years old.

Then one day, she called him up and said, "I think I'm going to move."

The sudden declaration caught him off guard, but he agreed when she explained her plan.

A real estate agent had introduced her to an apartment in ●●●●●, and she'd decided she liked the place.

The large house where she currently lived required a lot of maintenance and only served to remind her of her late husband. She wanted to spend her remaining days somewhere new, and if she lived in an apartment, she could ask her neighbors for help if she ever needed it. Her reasons made a lot of sense.

A checked the internet and found that the multibuilding apartment complex had been built in the eighties, during a suburban development boom, and had originally been quite popular with families. By now, most of the units had been converted into rental properties, and it was primarily inhabited by elderly couples and single people like his mother. What's more, the rent was quite cheap considering the square footage.

The apartment was located on ground carved out of a mountainside, but it was close to town and the incline his mother would have to traverse if she wanted to go shopping was gentle and wouldn't tax her elderly legs.

But when the real estate agent gave them a tour, A's impression was that the place seemed "depressing."

It had a lovely view of the town below, and the mountain behind the complex added a sense that nature wasn't far away. But everything about the place felt gloomy, probably because so few people lived there. The huge complex contained many buildings, but the sidewalks and park were deserted. Curtains decorated less than half the windows, and A guessed that fewer than 30 percent of the units were occupied. The flower beds and shared areas didn't look maintained. In fact, the place seemed almost abandoned, which only made it feel gloomier.

In contrast to A's uncertainty, his mother took a shine to the apartment immediately. She was pleased with the nice views and the natural setting.

She even liked the lack of other tenants. She was a quiet person, and crowds tended to tire her out.

So A held his tongue, figuring it was best for his mother to live in a place she liked.

They toured several units before she decided on a third-floor apartment in Building Five. The ten-story structure offered more options, but a higher floor would have meant more trouble going up and down. The real estate agent strongly recommended Building Five because its floor plans were more catered to single people and couples without children, allowing A's mother to make friends more easily. A's mother agreed.

But when she and A went around to meet the neighbors on the day she moved in, only one person on her floor answered—a surly old man who curtly accepted the snacks they'd brought, then promptly shut the door.

A couldn't shake his uneasiness. Was it really a good idea for his mother to be living in a place like this?

About half a year after his mother moved, a pipe cracked at A's apartment in Nagano. The leak was directly above his room, damaging the whole thing. Management informed him they would need a couple of days to replace the wallpaper and get everything repaired. Without a place to sleep, he saw an opportunity to take some time off work and to visit his mother at her apartment.

His job had kept him extremely busy since her move, so he hadn't been to see her in a while. She sounded elated when he called her and made the suggestion.

A hadn't seen the apartment since his mother moved in, and he found it just as depressing as before.

But when he got to his mother's room, he saw she'd hung up a calendar and there were more books on her bookshelf—ones she'd clearly bought after the move. It seemed to A like his mother had built a foundation from which to start her new life. He was also relieved to hear she'd gotten to know some of the other residents, despite their small number.

* * *

A's mother was a gentle woman who was always smiling.

She'd been that way for as long as A could remember. Back when he was young, A used to tell her about his days at school. She never said much in return, but she would listen to all his stories with a bright smile on her face. She was the complete opposite of his stern, unapproachable father.

When he got to her apartment, A found her sitting in a chair by the window, curtains pulled back to let in the sunshine. She listened to his news with a content smile.

But she seemed somehow different from the mother he knew. Every so often, as they talked, she'd twist her face into a strange expression.

As she nodded along to A's words, her smile would occasionally morph into a wide, toothy grin. Though she was still smiling, it almost seemed forced. Something about it reminded him of that same depressing sensation he'd felt the first time he toured the apartment. A asked his mother about it, but she seemed unaware that it was happening.

She would also spend long hours sitting in her chair and looking out the window, simply staring at the mountain view. Though his introverted mother preferred reading to going out, A thought it odd that she would sit there, without the TV on or any music playing, doing nothing but gazing out the window. As much as he hated to consider it, he suspected she might be developing dementia.

He had to ask.

"Why do you look out the window so much? Are there rare birds around here or something?"

Her eyes still glued to the view outside, his mother replied:

"I'm waiting."

A asked what she was waiting for, but she simply continued to smile without saying anything.

* * *

That evening, his mother said from the kitchen, "I'm going to make meat-and-potato stew. I have some persimmons for dessert in the fridge, too. You love stew and persimmons, right?"

A certainly adored meat-and-potato stew, but he'd never much cared for persimmons. Plus, it was spring. Persimmons weren't in season. He felt sad, thinking his mother's memory must be beginning to slip.

Despite his concerns, A's mother finished cooking and filled the table with food.

There was meat-and-potato stew, miso soup, sautéed baby broccoli, glass noodle salad, and freshly cooked rice. All were dishes A loved, and that only made him sadder.

But as soon as he took a bite, his mind blanked. None of the food had any flavor.

A change in the flavor of someone's cooking is a well-documented sign of dementia. But this seemed a little different. The meat-and-potato stew looked completely normal, but it had no taste whatsoever. He felt like he was chewing sand. If his mother had mistaken sugar for salt, the food might taste bad or strange. But it didn't taste bad; it was *completely flavorless.*

His mother kept eating the food on her plate, oblivious to her son's shock and dismay. But rather than enjoying her meal, she looked like she was tackling a chore.

A made a decision right then and there. He couldn't let his dear mother live like this. He would have her move in with him instead.

He set down his chopsticks as he considered how to broach the topic. That was when he heard a loud sound outside.

It was a peculiar noise, like a thud and a crash at about the same time.

Surprised, A ran to the window. His mother, however, moved with unusual speed and beat him there.

Down below, he saw the body of a person twitching in a pool of blood, their arms and legs bent at odd angles.

* * *

A's mother was a gentle woman who was always smiling.

A would never forget that moment.

His mother was staring down at the scene below, smiling contentedly.

After that, A sent her to live with some relatives until he could arrange for her to settle in with him. As he watched the moving truck take her things from the apartment and set off toward his house, a middle-aged woman called out to him from the park attached to the complex.

She introduced herself as someone from another building who knew his mother. The other day, she had noticed A going in and out of his mother's room. So when she saw him outside, she'd decided to approach him.

She'd met A's mother shortly after she moved in while walking in the park. There weren't very many people living in the apartment complex, so opportunities to meet others were limited. The woman said she always kept an eye out for A's mother but hadn't seen her recently. It seemed she hardly went outside anymore.

A informed her that his mother was moving and thanked her for looking out for her.

The woman replied, "I'll miss her, but I think it's for the best. I feel better knowing that she'll be living with her son. She shouldn't stay in a place like that…"

Apparently, it wasn't the first time someone had committed suicide there. It turned out that a number of people jumped off the roof of Building Five every year. Among certain circles, it was quite notorious.

The jumpers weren't people living in the apartment complex, either. Most of them came from far away just to end their lives. For some reason, it only happened at Building Five, so the other residents tended to keep their distance.

A was shocked to find out his mother had been living in such a place.

Just then, something occurred to A, and he asked if there had been any other suicides since his mother had moved in.

Apparently, two people had already jumped to their deaths. In other words, his mother had witnessed three suicides since moving in.

When he heard that, A was convinced.

His mother had been waiting. Sitting there by the window, she had been waiting for someone to jump.

She lives with him in Nagano now, always staring out the window with a blank expression on her face, as if waiting for something to happen.

Published in July 2008
in a Certain Monthly Magazine

Closing In On the Truth About the Mysterious Sticker!

Have you heard of the "mysterious sticker" that's been making the rounds on the internet lately?

Our readers have been asking us to look into it for a while, and our editorial team has finally decided to uncover the truth.

• The Mysterious Sticker

Start by looking at the picture. It shows a white square, ten centimeters on each side, with an indescribable human figure standing underneath a large black torii. The figure most closely resembles the popular image of Tsuno Daishi, or the Great Horned Master, featured on protective talismans from Enryaku Temple on Mount Hiei. Though the figure has no horns, its bizarrely long limbs and abstract style give off an ominous aura. And in each corner of the sticker is the character for *woman*, 女.

Lately, these creepy stickers have inexplicably been appearing all over the place.

• Distribution

Our editors hit the streets and found these stickers all around Tokyo, mostly on utility poles and walls. We also discovered some on the bottom of public mailboxes, on the windows of abandoned buildings, and in many other locations hidden from view. With this in mind, it seems unlikely the stickers are primarily meant to get people's attention.

The stickers aren't copies. Instead, the same image has been drawn by hand with either a pen or a brush, and the details and styles vary.

We also scoured the internet for clues. The phenomenon is widespread enough to have warranted dedicated threads on various forums, and a group of internet sleuths has suggested creating a distribution map covering the whole country.

According to the thread, the stickers can be found throughout Japan, from Hokkaido to Okinawa, but most have been spotted in western Japan.

• A Specialist's Opinion

Our editorial team felt that the design might have religious significance and wondered if the sticker could function as some kind of talisman, so we reached out to a university professor who specializes in religious studies.

The following was their response:

"I am not aware of any talismans like this one. Since it depicts a torii, I expect it's connected to a shrine rather than a temple. Talismans typically have more than just an image, though. They usually contain text with the name of the god being invoked, or the shrine they came from. This sticker only has the character for 'woman' in the corners. And this humanoid figure… I've never seen anything like it before. As you noted, it does resemble Tsuno Daishi. But in my opinion, it looks like an original creation, rather than an attempt to re-create an image of Tsuno Daishi. My assumption is that an amateur was attempting to create a protective talisman with some purpose in mind."

• Testimonies

Our editorial team managed to interview several people with knowledge of the stickers. Here is what they told us:

Testimony of O (fifty-two, male, security guard)

* * *

I was assigned to the headquarters of a major company. I won't tell you the name, but you've definitely heard of it. I worked the day shift, and a coworker and I took turns checking the entrances and the parking lot.

One day, the building sent a request to my security company. They asked us to tighten our patrols because somebody had done something to the walls.

They were talking about this sticker. Someone had stuck a bunch of those creepy stickers on the walls of the building. Some were about hip height, while others were way lower, and still others were high enough that we couldn't reach them without standing on tiptoe. All four walls had been vandalized.

Following that request, we would peel off the stickers whenever we found one. If we just tore them off, it would leave some residue, so we had to be careful. It was a real pain. The janitors removed them every single day. And it wasn't only that building, either. People found them in parks and on the walls of restaurants in the area, too.

But how should I say it...? It seemed like the stickers were put up randomly. Whoever did it wasn't trying to display them—they just wanted to put them up. Maybe they were marking territory, or something like that.

When more stickers appeared on our building, it felt less like harassment or some kind of prank, and more like they were simply compensating for the ones we'd peeled off.

The weird thing is we never saw anyone putting them up. We would just find them.

After the request, we increased our rounds. This was our job, after all. We even started checking the area around the building. But the stickers kept appearing.

I was transferred soon after, so the rest of this is stuff I heard from a coworker. The stickers continued after I left. It never stopped, so the building installed extra security cameras outside.

The day the security company installed them, they had someone from both the day and the night shift sit in the monitor room and watch the camera feeds, including the new ones. But the guards didn't see anything. The next day, however, when my coworker clocked in to take over for the night shift, a huge commotion had broken out.

There was a sticker on the outside of one of the second-floor windows. Even three grown men standing on each other's shoulders couldn't reach that high. A morning janitor had found it. From inside the building, it just looked like a white square, but when the sunshine hit it from the other side, it became clear it was one of those stickers. The janitor was terrified. Apparently, none of the security cameras monitored the second floor directly, but footage from other cameras in the area was examined, and nothing suspicious was found.

Testimony of T (forty-eight, male, reporter)

This happened in 2003, when I was covering a story about a family in Saitama that went missing (*see Editor's note).

It was a really strange case. The editorial department was amazed that an entire family of four could have been spirited away. The police must have considered it a potential criminal case, because they refused to release any information about it. I really struggled to find any leads. The story dominated the news at the time, and every newspaper was desperate to get their hands on even the tiniest bit of info.

I was the same. I rarely do this anymore, but back then, I was working day and night to gather information. Then a detective I'd known for a long time let something slip.

"That case is really creepy. If possible, I'd rather not get involved."

I thought he might be about to give me a big scoop, but I was wrong.

I begged him for leads, but all I got were little details about the strange state of the family's house.

Plenty of reports had mentioned that the family seemed to have vanished into thin air, but apparently that wasn't the only strange thing about the case.

* * *

The family had left their half-eaten breakfast on the dining room table. Beside the table was a couch facing a TV, with a low table in between. When they weren't eating, the family probably spent most of their time in the area with the sofa and the TV—a very common arrangement. But it was the low table that caught the investigator's attention.

He said there were four bundles of square paper on the table. Each stack was about ten centimeters tall, so roughly two hundred sheets. Beside the bundles of paper were four pens.

All the papers had the same design drawn on them: a *torii* with a person underneath.

It would make sense to assume the family was all drawing the same design on the pieces of paper. But think about it. The youngest daughter was only three years old. It's hard to believe she had the skill or patience to draw the same design two hundred times in a row. And no one understood why they were doing any of this to begin with.

When I heard that, I suspected the disappearance might be some sort of religious incident. I checked around, but I couldn't get a picture of the drawing, and I couldn't find any talismans or religions that used the image of a person underneath a torii.

My boss forbade us from publishing anything linking the case to religion unless we had hard evidence, so we never wrote anything about it.

When I heard the recent rumors about this sticker, I wondered if it was related. But I never saw the design that the family drew, so I can't say for certain.

**Editor's note:*

"In 2003, a family went missing in Kawagoe City, Saitama. One night, a man working in Tokyo called E (38), his wife (36), their eldest daughter (7), and their youngest daughter (3) all disappeared. Their unfinished breakfast was left in the house, and no coworkers, friends, or relatives heard anything from them. They had no known reason to leave, and though it was widely

reported on at the time, no explanation for their disappearance ever surfaced. It is now July 2008, and their whereabouts are still unknown."

Testimony of F (twenty, female, university student)

Chain e-mails used to be popular at the all-girls high school I attended. They're really common, right? You know, things like "If you don't send this picture to three people, something bad will happen to you."

One of those e-mails was really similar to the picture on the sticker. I couldn't believe it when I saw the stickers around the city after I started college.

But the sticker was a little different. It had the character 女, for *woman*, on each corner, but the one from the e-mail had the character 了, as in *end*. I remember talking to some friends about what it could possibly mean, so it stuck in my mind.

That chain e-mail was kind of unusual. It had a picture like the one on the sticker, but the accompanying text was really bizarre. This was a long time ago, so I don't remember it exactly, but it was something like this:

"Thank you for finding me. Send this to as many people as you can, and you will make a lovely friend. They're very cute."

Creepy, right? We all sent the text to one another as a joke, but one girl in our class who had a good sixth sense said it was really dangerous and that we should get rid of it, so I deleted it from my inbox.

Testimony of K (forty-five, female, housewife)

My friend went insane because of this sticker. Please be careful.

R was my neighbor, and our families used to spend time together. I'm a housewife because I have to take care of my kid, but R didn't have any children, and she and her husband both worked full-time. Even so, we would see each other while taking out the garbage, and she was always nice to me. I sometimes went over to her house. We were very close.

One day, I was over at R's house. She had the day off, and we hadn't seen each other in a while, so she'd invited me to tea. We were chatting about this and that, when R mentioned she had recently gotten into something new.

She sold insurance door-to-door and usually walked or rode her bicycle. She covered a lot of ground every day and knew her territory really well. One day during her rounds, she noticed that sticker all over town.

At first, she just thought, *Oh, there it is again*, whenever she saw one, but at some point, she started to enjoy finding them. Some had been placed in really obscure locations, so looking for them felt kind of like a treasure hunt. Spotting one would bring her a little burst of joy, so she'd keep an eye out while she made her rounds.

Her husband even teased her, telling me with a wry grin, "Isn't my wife such a weirdo?"

But the next time R talked to me about it, I began to wonder if there might be something wrong with her.

She'd made a map of all the places she'd found a sticker, and she was getting really worked up about it. She went on and on about how many she'd found, where they'd been, and which areas she planned to search next. She was very dedicated to her job, so I figured it made sense she was passionate about her hobbies as well. At the time, I just listened without giving it too much thought. But looking back now, I think she was already starting to lose it.

Later, R died.

She committed suicide.

On one of her days off, she suddenly announced that she was going to ●●●●●. She went there alone and jumped off the side of the dam.

I attended her funeral, but I couldn't bring myself to look at her husband. He was so distraught.

I remember running into him following the memorial service marking the forty-ninth day after her death. I hadn't seen him since the funeral, so I asked him how he was doing. He smiled as he spoke, his voice slow and calm.

He said that once he could function again, he started cleaning up R's belongings. He hadn't even been able to touch them for some time. But going through her things was really hard on him.

Just seeing her vanity table made him miss her. They'd brought it over from her parents' house, and she'd always loved it.

The vanity's three-paneled folding mirror had stayed closed since R's death. Remembering her sitting in front of it as she put on makeup, he began to think that maybe if he sat in front of it himself, it might help him understand her decision. He addressed her silently as he opened the doors.

The mirror was covered in those stickers. They were plastered over every inch of all three panels.

For a while, her husband simply sat there, staring at it. When he caught his reflection in a gap between two stickers, he realized he was smiling.

He moved away shortly after we spoke, leaving all his household belongings behind, as if he'd fled in the night.

As you can see from these four testimonies, the sticker appears to put a kind of curse on people. Perhaps they are being spread by some supernatural force. Any reader who finds one around town should be careful not to get too close.

The third testimony raises the possibility that the picture can spread through any medium. Interestingly, the image appears to vary as well.

If someone with evil intentions is using multiple avenues to spread this curse, then it could well pose a serious threat.

The editorial team will continue looking into this mysterious sticker. Please keep an eye out for future reports!

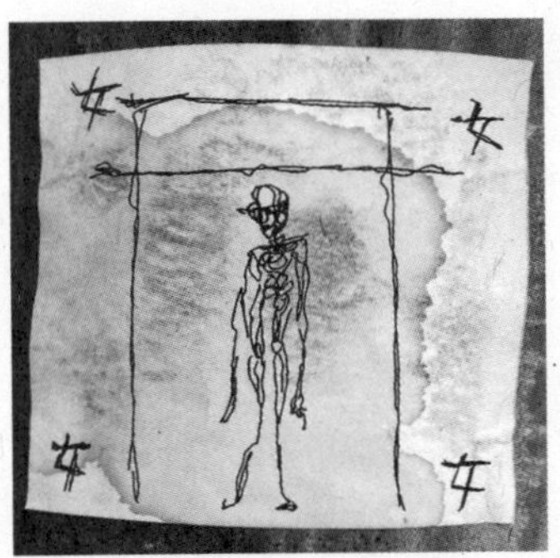

A picture of the sticker found during the editorial team's investigation. Could multiple people be trying to spread the same entity?

About a Place in the Kinki Region 3

"Everything's so disjointed..."

Ozawa's muttering contrasted with the delighted face on my computer screen.

After our previous meeting, we started e-mailing each other anytime one of us uncovered something.

Ozawa had suggested that rather than discussing each new piece of evidence, it might be more helpful to wait until we'd reached a point where we could examine our findings in depth. Two weeks later, we'd collected enough information to warrant an online meeting.

While virtual meetings like this have become more frequent since COVID, I still feel a little weird about not seeing someone in person. As I watched Ozawa deftly sharing his screen and speaking without any hesitation, I began to feel the gap in our ages.

"Complicated stories can be really enjoyable for readers. Personally, I'm quite fond of mysteries like this one, too," he added with a laugh. "It's fun to try to solve them."

We started by going over all our information.

It seemed Ozawa had been correct about mysterious incidents radiating out from the mountain, but more than one type of incident appeared to be involved.

We created broad categories, such as "the mountain caller," "the red woman," and "the cursed sticker."

In ●●●●●, people seemed to encounter the mountain caller on the west side of the mountain, and the red woman on the east side.

Once we'd settled all of that, we examined each story in turn.

"The biker's blog is probably related to the mountain caller we've seen in other creepy stories. The description of the shrine matches the one in *A Peculiar Comment* and the *Letter from a Reader Being Stalked*. Plus, the presence of the female dolls matches up with the obsession with women we see in the other stories."

At that point, I raised some issues that had been bothering me.

For some time, I'd more or less assumed all the incidents stemmed from a very powerful god whose shrine had fallen into ruin and who had lost all their worshippers. But the *hokora* in the biker's blog was filled with dolls. Shrines like that usually house gods, but this one didn't seem to contain the shrine's primary deity. So what had it originally held, and why wasn't it there now? Was there some reason it had gone missing? Or was there never anything inside to begin with?

"We'll have to search through the region's historical records, or else ask someone who knows about the place's history. Otherwise, it's going to be very tough to learn more about that shrine. And when it comes to the *hokora*, I doubt much detailed information on its origins has survived… There's nothing about it on the internet, and neither it nor the ruined shrine are named on any maps."

Ozawa's statement brought an end to the discussion, and we moved on to the next topic.

The red woman appeared in *A House to Rent* and in the interview about the cursed video. The woman in the *Letters to the Editor* section had the same characteristics. Details tend to be exaggerated as stories spread, but I figured it was safe to assume these were all the same woman.

However, these stories about the red woman involved a lot of unknowns. Ozawa described her behavior as "inexplicable," and I agreed. Why was she jumping? What was she feeling? We had no idea what was driving her.

"The mountain caller tries to lure people to the mountain, but the red woman goes out and approaches her targets. She seems to want them to find her. But we need more information. I'm so glad you interviewed K, the magazine's former editor. I couldn't have gotten in touch with him on my own. I'd appreciate it if you kept using your network to gather more info."

I nodded along silently, thinking about the college student from that interview. What was he doing now? Had the woman followed him?

Next, we talked about the ghost apartments on the east side of the mountain.

"This is the complex that appeared in *Masshiro-san.* And it shows up thirty years later in *Waiting*, where it has barely any residents. But based on the *Letter from a Reader Being Stalked*, Building Five was already a famous suicide spot some decades after the apartments went up. We can't yet say whether that was the cause of the complex's decline, or just a contributing factor."

His tone seemed to imply something, so I asked him to clarify, and he continued.

"I'm sure you've already realized this, but when I found the unpublished draft of *Waiting* among the research materials, I noticed something. The published article dropped the description of the building's surroundings, but the draft mentions that a mountain was visible from the windows of Building Five. That's right—our mountain."

With that, he shared an aerial photograph he got from the internet.

"The mother in the story spent every day watching the mountain from her window. Of course, if you only consider the story in isolation, it sounds like she was waiting for someone to throw themselves off the building. But we know there's something strange about that mountain, adding a new perspective on what the mother might have been waiting for."

I then brought up the part where she offers the narrator persimmons, as further support for Ozawa's theory.

Assuming the story was somehow related to the mountain caller, that could explain why people only jumped from Building Five. If you took the aerial photo and drew a straight line from the apartment complex to the small, isolated structure visible on the mountain (in other words, the ruined shrine), then Building Five would be the closest structure to the shrine in the complex.

In *Waiting*, the mother and son looked out the window and saw the body of the jumper. Unless it was random coincidence, this would mean the jumpers were choosing the closest spot atop the closest roof to the shrine, then leaping toward it.

Perhaps those on the west side of the mountain jumped from the dam, while those on the east side jumped off the roof of the apartment building.

"Building Five comes up in the interview about the cursed video as well. It's unknown when that video was recorded, but the red woman appears in it, too. I wonder if she and the mountain are connected somehow."

Ozawa was muttering to himself, fully aware that I couldn't answer his question.

"The sticker is as much of a mystery as the red woman."

I, too, had been baffled when Ozawa sent me *Closing In On the Truth About the Mysterious Sticker!*

The torii in the image, as well as the fact that one of the people in the testimonials went all the way out to the dam in ●●●●● to kill herself, seemed to imply there was some sort of connection. But the reason for the multiple designs remained a mystery.

"If the human figure on the sticker is the mountain caller, then the 'woman' character (女) in the corners kind of makes sense. But I don't understand the 'end' character (了) at all. It can be pronounced as 'ryou' and can indicate that something has ended or been completed. And the text in the chain e-mail with this character resembles the message from the red woman in *A House to Rent*. Of course, the woman said she didn't remember the words exactly, so it could just be a coincidence."

As he continued, I pondered whether the two varieties of sticker might serve different roles, or whether the change came about during the process of their creation.

"I did some investigating on my own after sending you that article. I walked around my neighborhood looking for the stickers, but I couldn't find any. I found a lot on the internet, though."

In fact, I had done the same thing, so I was well aware of how the cursed stickers had spread all over the internet.

Using an image search, I checked for any sites that had the cursed sticker, and I found quite a few.

The sticker appeared in multiple formats, such as on a random post in the middle of a forum thread, or from social media accounts that did nothing but post the image over and over again. Someone was obviously trying to spread the image online. I found both the 女 and 了 variants.

"It's kind of unnerving to find out the same image has been spreading through all sorts of different means for so many years."

A moment later, Ozawa added, "Honestly, when I read the article about the cursed sticker, I remembered hearing something similar from one of my friends in college..."

Then he told me the following story.

******

Back in college, Ozawa had a friend called E who was in the same major; E told him about a picture.

He'd said it was a drawing that depicted "something like a torii."

* * *

E was a pure, innocent country boy who had moved from the Tohoku region to Tokyo for college.

His student ID number was close to Ozawa's, so they had plenty of chances to talk with each other from day one. They even hung out around town together every now and then.

This story happened in the fall of the year I met Ozawa.

Now in his second year, E had become more cosmopolitan and had even dyed his hair brown. One day, he approached Ozawa in the cafeteria during lunch.

"I joined an entrepreneurs' club. I plan to start my own business after graduation."

E told Ozawa how he had been recruited at a café near campus. A couple sitting at the table next to his asked for a recommendation on a restaurant in the area, and the conversation progressed from there. They commented on E's keen business sense and invited him to join their club.

As E spoke animatedly about his future prospects, Ozawa realized that a pair of city dwellers were aiming to hoodwink his naive friend.

He explained they would most likely demand exorbitant membership fees and then try to lure him into a multilevel marketing scheme that would ruin him, but E didn't listen.

Instead, E began pressuring Ozawa to attend one of their meetings, declaring that once he joined, he'd see the club's obvious benefits.

Unable to stop his friend, Ozawa began to distance himself from E, praying that the club was somehow an honest enterprise.

But Ozawa didn't have to worry about avoiding E, because for half a year, he didn't see him on campus even once. It seemed he was hardly attending classes anymore.

Ozawa eventually ran into him at a convenience store near campus.

At this point, his friend looked quite haggard. The first words out of E's mouth when he saw Ozawa were:

"I was wrong. They were dangerous."

E had relished every activity the club offered.

They hosted seminars where actual CEOs revealed the secrets to their success, and study sessions designed to help members realize their full potential. Before joining, E had been attending college every day without any purpose or direction. But after he joined the club, his outlook had changed completely. He stopped prioritizing his classes, and his life began to revolve around the club.

Most of the members were university students like E who all shared the same passion for the club. E loved spending time with them, discussing their dreams for the future.

A few months into that life, an executive approached E.

The man invited E to a special party that only select members could attend. The club's leader, who was a board member at a big company, was going to host the party at his own home.

E immediately accepted. If he could impress the club's leader, it would help launch his future career.

When he arrived at the director's house, E had to pinch himself.

The man lived in the penthouse of a towering condominium in a classy part of Tokyo. Inside was a spacious living room decorated with expensive furniture, including a large table covered with succulent catering. A separate room was dedicated to the leader's art collection, and it was overflowing with strange objects, paintings, and art pieces that E had a hard time guessing the value of.

A few more than ten attendees stood around the room, glasses in hand as they discussed business. E couldn't believe he'd been invited to attend such an event, and he was full of excitement.

* * *

Roughly two hours later, the lights suddenly dimmed, and a projector's beam filled a large white wall to one side of the room.

The other partygoers immediately burst into a round of applause, so E assumed some regular event was about to start.

As everyone watched, a picture appeared on the wall.

It was an abstract drawing of a black torii that looked like an amateur's sketch, so E assumed it was some kind of artwork.

Everyone cheered. Then, after a short silence, they all began to speak at once, bathed in the light of the projector.

"Ruki emu dojie uzume"
"Meshi taga haha aoeoizu memi ochikudo"
"Zogi tsufuie hamo sumo ooe"
"Airuzu mesoudzu jiemifu oporeru tozue"
"Doiishime koyoi asu pikuso"
"Suei mikururu rueoki munashi"
"Aoie fuzumodzui seroo aburuiso"
"Chimemi fuzuroite tottusumo iteto bunaru ike komiteru"
"Fueo iepushi"
"Ritsu fuitoto mina oi oerutsu"
"Shikoe ributsui tote mizu"

E had no idea what was happening.

Paying E no mind, the others continued to blabber gibberish to one another as though it all made perfect sense.

Something far beyond E's understanding was unfolding before him.

Scared senseless, E roused his courage and tried saying something to the person closest to him.

Every member of the vociferous crowd went silent and stared at him.

The only sound in the room was the hum of the projector as a sea of blank faces stared at E through the faint light.

Each set of eyes observing him were empty, hollow, and lacked any hint of emotion.

Unable to contain his fear any longer, E dashed out of the room and went home.

The following day, he received a text from the club's leader, the man who had invited him to the party.

"Thank you for attending yesterday. It was such a great party. I'm sure it was a good experience for you, too."

The message made it sound like nothing had happened, so for a second, E wondered if he had somehow imagined it all. But the memory of his fear was so vivid that E couldn't dismiss it as a dream, and he cut ties with the club.

A month or so later, just as his nerves had finally begun to settle, he came back to his apartment from his shift at work to find a white paper attached to his door. It was the picture from the party.

From that day forward, no matter how many times he tore the paper off, it would return.

It haunted him, driving him to insomnia.

One sleepless night, as E tossed in bed, he heard a small noise from the direction of the front door. He turned toward the sound and saw the mail slot creak open.

A pair of eyes peered in at him from outside.

Their dull glint reminded E of the gazes of those people at the party.

The eyes stared straight ahead, motionless, but clearly observing him.

He held their gaze for what seemed like an eternity, before the mail slot closed and he heard footsteps slowly receding into the distance.

The next morning, the picture was back on his door.

******

"The picture in E's story only has a torii. But the way it keeps coming back and the image of the torii both match the sticker."

After finishing this tale, Ozawa continued, as if trying to lighten the mood.

"Well, even if someone is spreading some kind of curse, we're not exorcists or saviors. Let's just focus on gathering more information. In his interview, K said that the most important thing for readers is enjoyment, and I agree. But I'd rather report the truth than make up a story that's only loosely based on reality. I hope you'll stick with me until the end."

Honestly, I didn't want anything more to do with this thing. The more I involved myself, the more likely it seemed I'd wind up in danger. That was how I felt, anyway. But I'd accepted the job from Ozawa, so I had to keep working…

Transcript of an Interview 2

Oh, sure. I'll take an iced coffee, too.

I haven't spoken with F in a long time, so I was surprised when he reached out to me about this. Yes. It seems like he's still freelancing.

This is an interview for the monthly magazine OOOO, right? Oh, it's no longer monthly?

Is that editor guy not coming today? Oh, it's been ten years, so I don't remember his name… That's it—it was K.

Huh? He quit? You don't say…

But anyway, why are you doing a follow-up interview for such an old story? I heard they never even published the article on my graduation research.

No, no, I'm not upset. That exorcist K introduced me to back then saved my life.

If it wasn't for his help, I wouldn't be here now, ten years later. Next year, I'm going to be a father. Can you believe it?

* * *

But, well, see… I probably shouldn't be saying this to someone I'm meeting for the first time, but honestly, I wouldn't have agreed if it wasn't F who asked.

K was kind of rude back then… Oh, no, no, no, don't apologize. You had nothing to do with it. And I know that kind of behavior is probably normal in his line of work.

I was desperate at the time. I'd experienced something truly terrifying. K offering to introduce me to an exorcist felt like a godsend. But to K, of course, I was just another person he had to work to get the story.

He pressed me on whether any of it had actually happened, hinting I might be lying to get attention. Then he said it wouldn't be interesting for his readers as it was and asked if it would be all right to embellish this or that part of the story. I didn't appreciate him treating such a horrific experience as fodder for entertainment, and it kind of upset me.

But—and I guess this should be obvious—if the scary stories in magazines like that are true, they must have all been horrible experiences for the ones going through them. I imagine people covering stuff like that get jaded after a while.

Ever since it happened to me, I've stayed away from anything horror-related.

Oh, I'm not saying that everyone who writes about that stuff is like K, of course. I can tell you're taking me seriously. So please forget about what I just said.

Yes, that's right. This all happened after the interview.

Exactly. I agreed to share my story in exchange for an introduction to an exorcist, or whatever they're called.

I don't really know much about that kind of thing, but K referred me to a temple near Tama that had a good reputation for handling the supernatural.

When I spoke to the priest there, I remember he sighed in resignation.

I frantically explained how my graduation research had caused that strange woman to appear at my apartment. I told him that I planned to move soon for a job, and that I wanted him to do whatever it took to make sure she didn't follow me.

The priest said he didn't sense any woman connected to me, so she most likely wasn't after me anymore.

But he warned me she had probably invited something even worse into my life, and that I might be in grave danger.

I immediately requested an exorcism, but the priest said my case wasn't that simple.

Purification rituals can dispel regular spirits, but something more powerful was haunting me. He said that in Shinto terms, it was something close to a god.

According to him, humans have no power over such entities, and a purification ritual would have no effect. He told me there was nothing he could do.

I'm embarrassed to admit it, but when I heard that, I began to cry. I begged him to help me.

Was my only option to simply wait until whatever it was killed me?

He looked deeply conflicted, but in the face of my pleading, he eventually sank into thought. After a while, he said this:

"Adopt some living creature and start taking care of it. I can't say for certain if that's really the best way, though. After that, you must decide what to do on your own."

Ready to try anything, I stopped by a pet shop on my way home.

I hadn't ever owned a pet before, so I asked the staff to recommend something suitable for a beginner. Eventually, I decided on some Japanese rice fish.

The employee suggested keeping small shrimp with them. Did you know they're good companion pets? When red cherry shrimp share a tank with Japanese rice fish, the shrimp eat any leftover food and keep the water clean.

In the end, I bought some fish, shrimp, rocks, and a little tank and went home.

* * *

A few days later, ready to start my first job, I moved out of student housing and into a cheap apartment for single people. The fish came with me, of course.

That's right. Nothing happened. I had followed the priest's advice, so I assumed the fish were protecting me from any evil spirits.

I think it was about a month after I started my new job.

I began seeing something strange. It took the form of a little boy.

I'd see him standing way off in the distance as I walked around town. I could tell he wasn't a living human. He looked like an ordinary elementary school kid in shorts and a T-shirt, but—how can I put it?—no one ever noticed him. It was like no one recognized that he existed, like I was the only one who could perceive him.

Sometimes he'd appear amid a crowd of people, or in the shadow of a telephone pole. One time, I even saw him standing on the roof of a building opposite my window at work.

He always looked at me with a blank stare, his head tilted like he had something he wanted to ask.

Yes, I was terrified. I'd never seen a ghost before. I'd heard about the woman, but I never actually saw her. Naturally, I called the temple for advice, and the priest said I'd be fine so long as I kept caring for another living creature. He didn't say anything else.

The boy never did anything to me. He only ever stared at me from a distance, so I decided to pretend he wasn't there.

When I was doing my graduation research, I'd spoken with someone who had a good sixth sense, and he'd told me it was usually best to ignore them, so that's exactly what I did.

Then one night, I came back home from work as usual.

I always remove my socks as soon as I get home. That night, I took them off and tossed them into the washing machine, then I walked through my one-room apartment, past the fish tank.

Something felt weird under my feet, so I looked down. The floor was wet, and I had stepped on more than just water.

It was one of the little shrimp.

Had it already been dead? Or did I kill it when I stepped on it? I wasn't sure.

There was a big pool of water on the floor. Half the contents of the tank had spilled out, and the remaining fish and shrimp were swimming around frantically in the leftover space.

There hadn't been any earthquakes, and I couldn't figure out why all that water was on the floor.

Maybe my clothes had caught on the tank as I was

leaving that morning, causing the water to splash out, and the little shrimp had gotten caught up in the spill.

I felt bad. The shrimp might be small, but it was still a living creature. So I prayed over it.

Looking back now, I think it all started that night.

The boy continued to stare at me from afar.

A month later, one of the fish died.

I woke up in the middle of the night to use the bathroom and found it floating in the toilet bowl.

At that point, I could no longer write it off as a coincidence.

But there were still lots of fish and shrimp left in the tank.

Nothing happened for a couple of months, but I still saw the boy.

One evening, I went to get dinner from the convenience store.

On my way back, I noticed the boy off in the distance.

He was standing in the middle of the road, head tilted under a streetlight.

I started to turn away, ready to ignore him as usual.

* * *

That's when he suddenly started running.

Straight toward me, feet smacking the pavement.

His face remained blank, but his head wobbled around as he ran.

Now that I think about it, he hadn't been tilting his head at all. He simply couldn't hold it up straight.

I ran home as fast as I could.

Thankfully, the convenience store was really close, and I hadn't locked the door when I went out.

I flung it open and ran inside. Then, just as I locked the bolt behind me, it started.

THUD THUD THUD THUD THUD THUD THUD THUD THUD THUD THUD THUD

He hammered wildly on the door.

He hadn't looked strong enough to pound that hard.

The flimsy door of my cheap apartment rattled horribly.

Just as I was thinking it would break if he kept beating on it, the sound suddenly stopped.

I stood there for some time, frozen to the spot.

A while later, still terrified, I cracked the door open to peek outside, but no one was there.

Instead, I found a large dead gecko, probably squished by the door.

The fish and shrimp in my apartment were still doing well, swimming around in the tank.

* * *

Later, I decided to shell out the money for an apartment that allowed any kind of pet.

Once I'd moved, I adopted another animal.

I got a hamster.

About a year later, it went into hibernation and never woke up.

Then I got a parakeet.

It lived for almost three years, but eventually, it slammed itself into a window, broke a wing, and died.

Then I got married, and we bought a house.

Last year, the cat we'd owned for six years vomited up blood and died.

My wife was really sad.

We have a dog now. A golden retriever puppy.

The boy? Yes. I still see him. He's actually right there, on the other side of the street through that window. He's looking this way. What, you can't see him? Of course not. Ha-ha.

Published in May 1998
in a Certain Monthly Magazine

New UMA Discovered! The White Man!

"I know somebody who saw a UMA."

One of the freelancers we work with tipped us off about H, the man who witnessed the UMA, so we reached out to him.

When H arrived at our appointment, I thought he looked like a totally average person. To be honest, that reassured me because it meant his account was more likely to be credible.

We at the editorial department receive lots of tips every day, but many turn out to be fake. Some people even claim to be aliens. Reading a letter like that after working all night trying to put together a piece of reporting can be enough to push a person over the edge.

(Please understand the editorial department is in no way denying the existence of aliens or UFOs. These are separate matters.)

At any rate, the fact that H looked like a regular guy filled me with relief. He'd passed the first test, in other words.

H was a thirty-five-year-old office worker living in Tottori and employed by a big company. You'd never guess he had any cosmic or otherworldly connections.

But six years ago, on a family camping trip, he caught sight of a UMA.

Regular readers of this magazine hardly need another explanation of UMAs, but we'll give a basic overview for any noobs (sorry!) picking this up for the first time.

UMA stands for Unidentified Mysterious Animal. As the name implies, it's a general term for any creature whose existence is still unproven.

Because it uses English words, most people assume the name originates from overseas, but it was actually coined in Japan. Everyone knows that UFO stands for Unidentified Flying Object, and in 1976, a famous Japanese sci-fi magazine came up with UMA as a similar-sounding acronym. As a side note, people in English-speaking countries call these creatures cryptids.

One of the most famous UMAs is the Loch Ness Monster, affectionately called Nessie. Back in the seventies, the Japanese media went crazy for Nessie, spawning all sorts of local varieties, such as Issie in Lake Ikeda. Unfortunately for Nessie, the people involved with the famous photo later admitted it was a hoax, leaving the creature's existence in doubt.

Other well-known UMAs include the large primate referred to as Bigfoot, mermaids (or sirens), and creatures called skyfish, which are said to rocket through the air at high speeds. As it happens, we covered that last creature a few years ago. Technically, the term UMA also includes aliens.

At this point, let's take a moment to focus on Japan. Very few creatures in this country are categorized as UMAs. There are a few famous ones everyone knows about, such as *kappa*, the serpentine *tsuchinoko*, and the giant *takitaro* fish made famous by a certain fishing manga. But few Japanese people have heard of any others.

It has been said that Japan has so few UMAs because we have yokai instead.

Most people would call a *kappa* a yokai. The same goes for the long cloth-like creature called *ittanmomen*, the one-eyed *hitotsume-kozo*, and *jinmenken*, the human-faced dog that gained popularity in Japan a decade or so ago.

However, as long as people have claimed to see these creatures, they can be said to count as UMAs.

So it's not that Japan doesn't have many UMAs of its own, but that we have long put such creatures into a different category—that of yokai.

* * *

Debating whether an unidentified animal or creature in Japan should be a UMA or a yokai, however, is as unproductive as arguing over whether Ryoko Hirosue is an actress or an idol.

Kappa don't care whether we call them UMAs or yokai. The media decides to portray them a certain way, and the public gradually comes to accept that portrayal. If you think about it, the media is the truly guilty party.

As the editor of a magazine focused on horror and the paranormal, I often fret over the best way to describe such creatures. But this time, in the hopes of spreading the term UMA in Japan, I have chosen to use that term for the remainder of this article.

Perhaps I spent a little too much time on that introduction. Allow me to finally introduce the UMA H witnessed firsthand.

H saw the UMA in the fall of 1992, at a campsite in ●●●●●.

He drove all the way there from distant Tottori for a one-night camping trip.

The campsite, aimed at motorists and nestled at the foot of a mountain near a dam, opened in 1985, just before the start of the camping craze. Initially, scores of young people jumped on the bandwagon, heading to the site to enjoy light hikes and other outdoor activities. Business boomed, and the place was filled to capacity even on weekdays.

H visited the campsite right at the height of the fervor. He was a vigilant observer of current trends and was especially excited to be doing something with his family. He bought a tent and a full complement of gear, and he'd already camped in several other places earlier that year with his family.

However, when they arrived at the campground that weekend, H and his family found it vacant, despite the nice location.

As a single person in their thirties who has no friends but does have a mind consumed by the paranormal, I cannot imagine why people would prefer an empty campground. But apparently when there is a crowd, those who camp with their family often run into problems with young people throwing late-night parties.

So H thanked his lucky stars and began setting up his tent with his wife, Y, and their son, M (who was six at the time). They then lit a fire and enjoyed the peaceful solitude.

Apparently, a woman's intuition can also detect UMAs. Y was the first to feel that something was amiss. She said her head hurt, and she kept glancing off into the distance. H asked what she was looking at, and she pointed across the dam to the mountain, saying she felt something watching them.

Then the radio started acting funny. There was nothing wrong with the signal, but now and then, they would hear a man's voice mixed in with the regular broadcast.

To H, it sounded like moaning. But M thought he heard it say something like "Heeey." And as soon as M said that, H began to hear it, too. It was very faint, but he could just make out the word.

More strange occurrences followed. The family all made curry together for dinner. M nervously helped cut vegetables and cook rice. But the food had no flavor. H first assumed that his taste buds had malfunctioned, but the rest of his family also tasted nothing. They'd used a store-bought curry mix, but he had a hard time believing a spicy dish like curry could turn out so bland.

At that point, M's nose suddenly started bleeding. It took a long time to stop, and they couldn't figure out what had caused it.

At this point, readers poisoned by our magazine's influence might be crying, "It's aliens!"

Radio wave interference, headaches, and bloody noses can all be the result of disruptions to electromagnetic fields. In other words, a UFO using electromagnetic field propulsion caused everything.

Our editorial team would like to refute that idea. Not because we've had our fill of UFOs, of course. We have several, concrete reasons.

First, there have been no recorded UFO sightings in the surrounding area. In Japan, most UFOs are witnessed multiple times in the same area, such as with the famous Kofu sighting. There is a theory that UFOs are restricted to certain flight paths due to variations in the earth's electromagnetic field. A single, isolated incident like this would be very peculiar.

Second, the campsite was a poor location for a UFO to touch down. Most UFOs are said to land in farms, fields, and other large, flat spaces. But H's campsite sat at the base of a mountain, surrounded by forested hills and a dam, without any open spaces. Even if those aboard the UFO simply intended to beam people up, they would have a hard time finding anyone among the trees.

Also, as will be described later, this UMA seemed to be very large. An alien of that size would require an enormous UFO to contain its massive body. This also makes the lack of eyewitnesses even more peculiar, and it's hard to imagine a giant UFO flying through the mountains with no place to land.

But let's return to H's story.

The string of mysterious events drained the family's enthusiasm, and they retired into their tent early to go to sleep for the night.

The next morning, Y told H something as he brushed his teeth at the washing station.

All night long, she'd heard someone outside their tent.

She swore she'd been able to make out a man's voice, mixed with the chorus of crickets, calling out "Heeey." But it had seemed to be coming from a long way away, so she hadn't bothered to wake up H.

What's more, she felt the same eyes from the day before staring at her from the mountain behind the dam, and the sensation terrified her.

H brushed it all off, however. They'd come all the way from Tottori, and he insisted they should enjoy themselves. That day, he and M hunted for bugs and explored the area around the dam while Y stayed inside the tent with a wretched headache.

Late that afternoon, just as they were packing their tent away in the car and preparing to leave, H remembered seeing a sign for an observation deck near the campsite. He decided to take his family there for a memorial photograph in front of the gorgeous view.

After climbing a flight of stairs, they arrived atop a wooden observation deck. The structure seemed to predate the campground considerably.

After gazing out at the scenery dyed in the colors of the setting sun, H was raising his disposable camera to snap a picture when M shouted and pointed into the distance.

He was pointing across the dam in the direction of the mountain. There, about five hundred meters away, they saw something white between the trees. It fluttered and waved in the wind like a cloth suspended from a tree branch.

The observation deck offered a couple of rust-covered binoculars—the kind that require a ten-yen coin to open the shutters.

M begged to try them, so H put a coin in the slot and held the boy up to the viewfinder. M began adjusting the focus to get a better look at the white object.

He stared intently through the binoculars for a while before suddenly bursting into tears.

Surprised, H passed the crying M to Y and looked through the binoculars himself.

The white object looked like a giant hand. Through the gaps in the trees, H could just glimpse the massive white body attached to it. The creature seemed to be naked and several meters tall.

Its hand was moving as if beckoning them closer.

H backed away from the binoculars as Y and M looked on, concerned. Just then, H realized something. The incessant cacophony of chirping crickets had stopped.

Unable to fathom this strange situation and the creature he had just seen, H hesitantly peered through the binoculars one more time. The hand was now pointing directly at him.

H claims he stayed transfixed by the hand for some time. He still doesn't know how long he stared. But once he recovered from his stupor, he backed away from the binoculars to discover that Y and M were gone.

Dashing down the stairs of the observation deck, he found his wife and son walking hand in hand toward the opposite side of the parking lot.

When he asked Y where they were headed, she simply said, "Let's go," over and over with a delirious grin.

H forced them into the car and drove away. They regained their senses a short while later, and neither remembered anything about the observation deck.

That is where H's story ends. Our editors have determined that his detailed account is not a fabrication.

No human-shaped white animal of that size currently exists in Japan. It seems unlikely it was merely a tall man pulling a weird prank, either. And no one else has ever come forward with another story of such a UMA. While there is a creature in Japan that is similar to North America's Bigfoot, they're a kind of yokai called *Iju*, and they look wholly different from what is described in H's testimony. Therefore, our editorial team has decided this is a brand-new UMA, and they've dubbed it the White Man.

The White Man imitates the speech and movements of humans, so unless the behavior is some kind of animal instinct, it may possess some degree of intelligence. The sirens of foreign legend sing to draw in sailors, and Japanese *kappa* imitate the cries of babies for similar reasons. Maybe the White Man possesses a related power.

Perhaps, like those other creatures, it seeks to steal the lives of humans (or their life force).

Our editorial team will keep gathering as much information as we can on the White Man. We are currently attempting to secure the funds to conduct field research. The future of our investigation depends on this magazine's sales, so we ask that you keep purchasing, dear readers!

Illustration based on H's testimony.
A large, white something points this way!

Letters to the Editor 2

I keep repeating myself, but you are no good. You, cruel and arrogant

Like my old neighbor Said   you are harmful

You know that microwaves are dangerous too. Don't you

I have been a receptor for a Long Long time but you do not have the ears to listen

You don't even try to receive it   before it is transmitted as Electricity, how utterly sinful

Those deep below the ground are crying   it's such a Shame,

and they still swim through this world like tuna   not aware of anything

Wearing human skins with wide smiles   are They imitating saints?

But   pretending to be human they have lost everything Inside of them long ago

The west was noisy again yesterday   The sound rang in my   ears   like the howling of Monkeys   ●●●●●

And they do nothing, but keep watch   as a group!!!!

Children Are always adorable. They have to be. You know that, right

Yesterday the noise from the calculator stopped at 9   In Two days' time, they might press 10

That's How far it's spread

We must kill the evil   Our master says so

Akira is evil   That Woman birthed it   But not from her womb   The demon, gave it power   Such a Shame

From far away. It used electricity to attack and Torture people   Then you spread your rumors and now it's over

The beauty of a bird soaring in the sky   It's   glorious!You can't do that with batteries

All the food contains poison, too. It does

That creature   in the mountain   only a shameless fool   would call it a go.d   . Its power made it a false god

Go be tricked by persimmons and things   if you choose

The bad one is   the demon

**The envelope was addressed to "The creators of ○○○○."*

It is believed to have been placed directly into the company mailbox.

The sender and date are unknown.

Information from the Internet 3

Excerpt from *Ultimate Threads: The Ultra-Terrifying Talisman House*

On January 15, 2011, a thread titled *Paranormal Hot Spots: Live Updates from Spooky Locations in the Kinki Region* appeared on an online forum.
The thread's original poster (Sergeant Kansai) claimed to live in the Kansai area and left his destination up to the replies.
In the end, he wound up going to the Talisman House in ●●●●●...

The following is a summary of that thread.

******

Paranormal Hot Spots: Live Updates from Spooky Locations in the Kinki Region

1: **Sergeant Kansai**: 01/15/2011 (Sat) 01:32:24
ID: H7cKvHk1c
I'm bored and wanna check out haunted spots in Kinki. Where's good?
I'm a guy in Kansai, and I have wheels.
Anyone wanna come with?

2: Anonymous: 01/15/2011 (Sat) 01:37:01
ID: fJf96cCp4
I'd love to, but I'm in Tokyo...

3: Anonymous: 01/15/2011 (Sat) 01:40:10
ID: gBbp5D2vd
Go to Inunaki Pass.

4: Anonymous: 01/15/2011 (Sat) 01:42:21
ID: c2rY89bq8
You've gotta check out the abandoned hotel on Mt. Maya.

7: Anonymous: 01/15/2011 (Sat) 01:42:58
ID: 4yjy8jlc
They say the area around my house is haunted.

9: **Sergeant Kansai**: 01/15/2011 (Sat) 01:50:09
ID: H7cKvHk1c
The replies will decide.
>>15

10: Anonymous: 01/15/2011 (Sat) 01:51:02
ID: Pxrbnij3U
My hometown has a paranormal hot spot.

12: Anonymous: 01/15/2011 (Sat) 01:52:34
ID: nHp7s7K3u
The year's barely started and you already have too much free time.

15: Anonymous: 01/15/2011 (Sat) 01:54:52
ID: Aylg8wLma
Talisman House in ●●●●●.

18: Anonymous: 01/15/2011 (Sat) 01:55:02
ID: fJf96cCp4
>>15
Where is it?

22: Anonymous: 01/15/2011 (Sat) 02:01:39
ID: gBbp5D2vd
>>18
Is this it?
Broken link

24: Anonymous: 01/15/2011 (Sat) 02:04:28
ID: nHp7s7K3u
I've seen it online before.
The inside is covered in talismans.

25: Anonymous: 01/15/2011 (Sat) 02:06:31
ID: vp6q6E2nc
My friend is from nearby.
It's just an abandoned house where some crazy lady used to live.

26: Anonymous: 01/15/2011 (Sat) 02:10:25
ID: gBbp5D2vd
So are you going, Sergeant Kansai?

34: **Sergeant Kansai**: 01/15/2011 (Sat) 02:33:16
ID: H7cKvHk1c
Sorry for the silence. I popped over to the convenience store.
Guess I'm going to Talisman House.
It's about a two-hour drive from here.
Anyone coming with?
I can pick you up if you're in Kansai.

35: Anonymous: 01/15/2011 (Sat) 02:35:24
ID: 4yjyf8jlc
I'm going!
jk

36: **Sergeant Kansai**: 01/15/2011 (Sat) 02:36:45
ID: H7cKvHk1c
>>35
How quickly you betray me lol.

39: Anonymous: 01/15/2011 (Sat) 02:40:01
ID: nHp7s7K3u
It's cold out there. Bundle up.

51: Anonymous: 01/15/2011 (Sat) 05:48:39
ID: fJf96cCp4
Will you give up if no one goes with? It's already morning.
I was looking forward to this.

60: Anonymous: 01/15/2011 (Sat) 07:33:19
ID: gBbp5D2vd
You dead, Sergeant?

71: **Sergeant Kansai**: 01/15/2011 (Sat) 09:12:58
ID: H7cKvHk1c
Sorry, I fell asleep.
Doesn't look like anyone is coming, so I'll just go by myself.
I'll upload photos.
Heading out now.

72: Anonymous: 01/15/2011 (Sat) 09:29:13
ID: fJf96cCp4
Good luck, Sergeant!

73: Anonymous: 01/15/2011 (Sat) 09:40:39
ID: gBbp5D2vd
Going ghost hunting in the morning? Gotta admit, that sounds pretty cool.

75: **Sergeant Kansai**: 01/15/2011 (Sat) 09:51:27
ID: H7cKvHk1c
I don't really go to abandoned buildings much. What do I need?

76: Anonymous: 01/15/2011 (Sat) 09:54:33
ID: nHp7s7K3u
Gloves, flashlight, and guts.

78: **Sergeant Kansai**: 01/15/2011 (Sat) 09:55:43
ID: H7cKvHk1c
>>76
OK.
I don't have a flashlight at home, so I'll get one.
I'll be driving, so I'll check in later.

79: Anonymous: 01/15/2011 (Sat) 09:56:59
ID: gBbp5D2vd
We'll hold down the fort while you're gone.

80: Anonymous: 01/15/2011 (Sat) 10:11:01
ID: 4dukJE2cm
Drive safe.

120: **Sergeant Kansai**: 01/15/2011 (Sat) 12:38:19
ID: H7cKvHk1c
I'm here.

121: Anonymous: 01/15/2011 (Sat) 12:45:20
ID: nHp7s7K3u
That was quick.

122: Anonymous: 01/15/2011 (Sat) 12:47:49
ID: fJf96cCp4
Glad you got there okay.

123: Anonymous: 01/15/2011 (Sat) 12:48:01
ID: gBbp5D2vd
Photos, please!

126: **Sergeant Kansai**: 01/15/2011 (Sat) 12:52:05
ID: H7cKvHk1c
Here's the outside.
Can you see it?
Broken link

127: Anonymous: 01/15/2011 (Sat) 12:52:59
ID: gBbp5D2vd
Wow, it just looks like a regular house.

128: Anonymous: 01/15/2011 (Sat) 12:53:04
ID: niH225uJb
Spooky...

129: Anonymous: 01/15/2011 (Sat) 12:53:44
ID: k8S24pg6z
I thought it was farther out in the country.

130: Anonymous: 01/15/2011 (Sat) 12:54:09
ID: fJf96cCp4
The grass is totally overgrown.

133: Anonymous: 01/15/2011 (Sat) 12:54:29
ID: 46bqFp2m9
How do you get inside?

135: **Sergeant Kansai**: 01/15/2011 (Sat) 12:55:24
ID: H7cKvHk1c
The front door is all boarded up. I'll look around for some way in.

139: Anonymous: 01/15/2011 (Sat) 12:56:12
ID: TurUk&v3
Reported you for trespassing (^ Д ^)

140: Anonymous: 01/15/2011 (Sat) 12:56:58
ID: gBbp5D2vd
>>139
Stop it.
You're killing the excitement.

142: **Sergeant Kansai**: 01/15/2011 (Sat) 12:58:03
ID: H7cKvHk1c
Some old lady is looking at me.
She must think I'm suspicious.

143: Anonymous: 01/15/2011 (Sat) 12:58:40
ID: Pxrbnij3U
Busted already lol.

162: Anonymous: 01/15/2011 (Sat) 13:10:23
ID: 7oZdFjgsv
Don't leave us hanging, Sergeant!

165: Anonymous: 01/15/2011 (Sat) 13:12:01
ID: fJf96cCp4
Hello?

168: **Sergeant Kansai**: 01/15/2011 (Sat) 13:13:08
ID: H7cKvHk1c
I was talking to the lady.
Here's a summary. It'll take a minute because I'm on my phone.

169: Anonymous: 01/15/2011 (Sat) 13:13:45
ID: gBbp5D2vd
OK! No rush. We're all waiting for your report.

193: **Sergeant Kansai**: 01/15/2011 (Sat) 13:32:58
ID: H7cKvHk1c
The old lady was eyeing me while I walked around the house, so I asked her about it.
Me: I'm studying this region for a college course. Is this house abandoned?
Lady: Yep.
Me: For how long?
Lady: Around ten years now, I'd say.
Me: Can you tell me anything about it?
Lady: Okay, but don't go sneaking in there. Lots of young'uns come out here to scare themselves and whatnot. Haven't seen many recently, though.
Me: I'll leave if you tell me the story.
Lady: Everyone 'round here knows it. A mother and her son used to live here. I don't think she was married. Friendly sort, the mother. She'd wave and say hello to you on the street. But then her kid passed. It was so sad. Apparently, he killed himself. At the time, they said it was 'cause of bullying. Reporters were crawling all over the front yard. They were yapping about it in all the magazines and on TV, but a lot of what they said was nothing but rumors. The mother started acting strange after that. Well, she was a bit of an odd duck even before the thing with her son. First she started talking nonsense. Then she killed herself, right here in this house. It's such a pity. She really loved her son. Must've torn her apart.

194: Anonymous: 01/15/2011 (Sat) 13:34:28
ID: Pxrbnij3U
You have good people skills for someone who lives online, Sergeant.

195: Anonymous: 01/15/2011 (Sat) 13:34:33
ID: q55ePRm52
What a development.

196: Anonymous: 01/15/2011 (Sat) 13:35:16
ID: 3trifSqnv
As expected of the media.

197: Anonymous: 01/15/2011 (Sat) 13:36:09
ID: gBbp5D2vd
Don't tell me you're just gonna leave.

205: **Sergeant Kansai**: 01/15/2011 (Sat) 13:39:47
ID: H7cKvHk1c
>>197
I'm not going anywhere.
The old lady is gone, so I'm checking the garden for a way in.

206: Anonymous: 01/15/2011 (Sat) 13:40:29
ID: fJf96cCp4
That's our Sergeant!

207: Anonymous: 01/15/2011 (Sat) 13:41:18
ID: gBbp5D2vd
If a bunch of idiots are going there for scares, there's gotta be some way inside.

208: Anonymous: 01/15/2011 (Sat) 13:42:09
ID: Aylg8wLma
Window.

209: Anonymous: 01/15/2011 (Sat) 13:43:01
ID: 3trifSqnv
Break down the door.

215: **Sergeant Kansai**: 01/15/2011 (Sat) 13:46:18
ID: H7cKvHk1c
Got in through a broken window.
It's really dusty.
The place is a mess.

216: Anonymous: 01/15/2011 (Sat) 13:47:04
ID: gBbp5D2vd
Pictures, please.

217: Anonymous: 01/15/2011 (Sat) 13:47:09
ID: 5tBqe2fQ6
Dying for pictures.

218: Anonymous: 01/15/2011 (Sat) 13:48:12
ID: fJf96cCp4
So excited.

222: **Sergeant Kansai**: 01/15/2011 (Sat) 13:51:25
ID: H7cKvHk1c
This seems like the living room.
It's dark, and I can hardly see anything.
Broken link

223: Anonymous: 01/15/2011 (Sat) 13:52:28
ID: icgCxssO8
There's still lots of stuff there.

224: Anonymous: 01/15/2011 (Sat) 13:52:58
ID: fJf96cCp4
Shouldn't it have talismans?

225: Anonymous: 01/15/2011 (Sat) 13:53:17
ID: gBbp5D2vd
Where are the talismans?

226: Anonymous: 01/15/2011 (Sat) 13:53:56
ID: nHp7s7K3u
It's more vandalized than it is messy.

227: Anonymous: 01/15/2011 (Sat) 13:54:19
ID: fJf96cCp4
It's kind of intense knowing someone killed themselves there.

228: **Sergeant Kansai**: 01/15/2011 (Sat) 13:55:04
ID: H7cKvHk1c
I don't see any talismans anywhere.
But there are loads of books and CDs like this.
Broken link

229: Anonymous: 01/15/2011 (Sat) 13:55:12
ID: 5tBqe2fQ6
Wow...

231: Anonymous: 01/15/2011 (Sat) 13:55:43
ID: e9wcVsbu
She was pretty out there, huh.

234: Anonymous: 01/15/2011 (Sat) 13:56:01
ID: gBbp5D2vd
A total nutjob.

235: Anonymous: 01/15/2011 (Sat) 13:56:34
ID: fJf96cCp4
So the mom was into New Age stuff?

236: Anonymous: 01/15/2011 (Sat) 13:56:57
ID: apV7ghO3m
No wonder her kid was bullied.

240: Anonymous: 01/15/2011 (Sat) 13:59:46
ID: nHp7s7K3u
Seriously, though, people with strong beliefs, even if it's about cosmic energy or New Age-y stuff, can leave behind a lot of residual energy when they die, making hauntings way more likely.

241: Anonymous: 01/15/2011 (Sat) 14:01:21
ID: 4yjyf8jlc
>>240
Thank you, Madame Psychic.

242: Anonymous: 01/15/2011 (Sat) 14:02:25
ID: gBbp5D2vd
So the talismans were just a rumor?

243: Anonymous: 01/15/2011 (Sat) 14:02:48
ID: Aylg8wLma
Tatami room.

245: **Sergeant Kansai**: 01/15/2011 (Sat) 14:03:56
ID: H7cKvHk1c
I just heard something.

246: Anonymous: 01/15/2011 (Sat) 14:04:49
ID: 8fdqKw5mx
What?

247: Anonymous: 01/15/2011 (Sat) 14:04:59
ID: fJf96cCp4
((((; ° Д °)))) *shudders*

248: Anonymous: 01/15/2011 (Sat) 14:05:18
ID: 8a29Mbdxi
Get out of there!

249: Anonymous: 01/15/2011 (Sat) 14:05:22
ID: gBbp5D2vd
Could it be the cops?

250: Anonymous: 01/15/2011 (Sat) 14:05:30
ID: 8fdqKw5mx
Everything okay?

251: Anonymous: 01/15/2011 (Sat) 14:06:03
ID: 4yjyf8jlc
Sergeant… RIP…

255: **Sergeant Kansai**: 01/15/2011 (Sat) 14:08:37
ID: H7cKvHk1c
I ran upstairs.
I heard a thunk through the wall when I was fishing around in the living room.

256: Anonymous: 01/15/2011 (Sat) 14:09:26
ID: s9sdW2boy
Abandoned spots like that are often owned by the yakuza, so don't push your luck.

257: Anonymous: 01/15/2011 (Sat) 14:10:05
ID: fJf96cCp4
Don't be afraid, Sergeant! Just head straight for the sound!

258: **Sergeant Kansai**: 01/15/2011 (Sat) 14:10:37
ID: H7cKvHk1c

I can still hear regular thumps coming from downstairs.
I'm gonna check out the upstairs for now.

259: Anonymous: 01/15/2011 (Sat) 14:11:11
ID: 9673gaMsj
Sergeant, you have balls of steel lol.

260: Anonymous: 01/15/2011 (Sat) 14:11:48
ID: tmXuQd2dt
Maybe you should leave.

262: **Sergeant Kansai**: 01/15/2011 (Sat) 14:13:24
ID: H7cKvHk1c
This looks like the kid's room.
Broken link

263: Anonymous: 01/15/2011 (Sat) 14:14:29
ID: gt4ohe95T
Whoa... So this is the room of the son who killed himself.

264: Anonymous: 01/15/2011 (Sat) 14:15:39
ID: gBbp5D2vd
I used to have that bear when I was a kid.

267: Anonymous: 01/15/2011 (Sat) 14:15:48
ID: Aylg8wLma
Desk drawers.

268: Anonymous: 01/15/2011 (Sat) 14:16:12
ID: fJf96cCp4
Looks like he was still in elementary school.

269: **Sergeant Kansai**: 01/15/2011 (Sat) 14:16:40
ID: H7cKvHk1c
There was a picture in the desk.
Broken link

270: Anonymous: 01/15/2011 (Sat) 14:17:29
ID: 6g79GpH4WXX
Aaaahhhhhhhhhhhhhhhhhh

271: Anonymous: 01/15/2011 (Sat) 14:17:52
ID: gBbp5D2vd
Is that the dead kid?

272: Anonymous: 01/15/2011 (Sat) 14:18:29
ID: fJf96cCp4
This is pretty scary.

273: Anonymous: 01/15/2011 (Sat) 14:18:40
ID: nHp7s7K3u
You gotta stop right now. This is bad news.

274: Anonymous: 01/15/2011 (Sat) 14:18:51
ID: k63mPvfqw
I'm terrified.

275: Anonymous: 01/15/2011 (Sat) 14:19:04
ID: t64dkyMnk
Why would the kid have a picture of himself in his desk?

276: **Sergeant Kansai**: 01/15/2011 (Sat) 14:19:55
ID: H7cKvHk1c
Doesn't look like there's anything else here.
And the noise has stopped, so I'll go back downstairs.

277: Anonymous: 01/15/2011 (Sat) 14:21:01
ID: pg3bZhYtu
You should probably leave now.

278: Anonymous: 01/15/2011 (Sat) 14:21:38
ID: gBbp5D2vd
You came this far, Sergeant. Let's see it all.

283: **Sergeant Kansai**: 01/15/2011 (Sat) 14:23:32
ID: H7cKvHk1c
I'm in the tatami room. I think the noise was coming from in here.
Broken link

284: Anonymous: 01/15/2011 (Sat) 14:24:20
ID: fJf96cCp4
Why is the center mat stained...?

285: Anonymous: 01/15/2011 (Sat) 14:24:58
ID: gBbp5D2vd
Someone definitely died in this room.

289: Anonymous: 01/15/2011 (Sat) 14:25:38
ID: nHp7s7K3u
This room is the worst one.

290: Anonymous: 01/15/2011 (Sat) 14:25:44
ID: pg3bZhYtu
What's that space in the left back corner?

291: Anonymous: 01/15/2011 (Sat) 14:26:50
ID: nHp7s7K3u
You should really get out of there right now.

293: Anonymous: 01/15/2011 (Sat) 14:27:05
ID: 4yjyf8jlc
Sergeant, you're a legend. Not one ounce of fear.

295: **Sergeant Kansai**: 01/15/2011 (Sat) 14:27:10
ID: H7cKvHk1c
>>290
It's a traditional room, so it's probably for the Buddhist altar.
But there's nothing there.

>>293
If I left now, you guys would never let me live it down.

296: Anonymous: 01/15/2011 (Sat) 14:27:56
ID: u4J2iskNr
Sergeant… You're the man.

297: Anonymous: 01/15/2011 (Sat) 14:28:09
ID: Aylg8wLma
Under the tatami.

299: **Sergeant Kansai**: 01/15/2011 (Sat) 14:29:00
ID: H7cKvHk1c
>>297

Yeah, the middle tatami is kinda raised up a little.
Wonder why.

301: Anonymous: 01/15/2011 (Sat) 14:29:31
ID: fJf96cCp4
It totally is.

302: Anonymous: 01/15/2011 (Sat) 14:29:55
ID: gBbp5D2vd
You gotta lift it up.

305: Anonymous: 01/15/2011 (Sat) 14:31:55
ID: DtDzw3z49
I've had enough.

306: Anonymous: 01/15/2011 (Sat) 14:32:17
ID: b3m8P28v9
Where are the talismans, anyway?

307: **Sergeant Kansai**: 01/15/2011 (Sat) 14:33:19
ID: H7cKvHk1c
>>302
I don't know if I can, but I'll try.
Glad I brought gloves.

>>306
I don't see any talismans.
But I see residue from stuff that was peeled off the beams, so something might have been there before.

308: Anonymous: 01/15/2011 (Sat) 14:33:51
ID: nHp7s7K3u
Seriously, you've gotta stop.

316: **Sergeant Kansai**: 01/15/2011 (Sat) 14:36:52
ID: H7cKvHk1c
What's this?
Broken link

317: Anonymous: 01/15/2011 (Sat) 14:37:48
ID: ss9pHX797
What the hell is that?

318: Anonymous: 01/15/2011 (Sat) 14:37:58
ID: gBbp5D2vd
A boulder? Or maybe just a big rock?

319: Anonymous: 01/15/2011 (Sat) 14:38:17
ID: fgso4pgV6
That looks like a sacred rope tied around it.
Think there's something enshrined in the rock?

320: Anonymous: 01/15/2011 (Sat) 14:38:26
ID: BeVis3d9h
Maybe someone put it there after the house was abandoned.

321: Anonymous: 01/15/2011 (Sat) 14:38:51
ID: fJf96cCp4
Wasn't the mother into New Age stuff?

323: Anonymous: 01/15/2011 (Sat) 14:39:03
ID: NPeHwjda4
This is too much… I'm terrified…

324: Anonymous: 01/15/2011 (Sat) 14:39:09
ID: nHp7s7K3u
Leave. Now.

325: Anonymous: 01/15/2011 (Sat) 14:39:16
ID: Aylg8wLma
Thank you very much.

326: Anonymous: 01/15/2011 (Sat) 14:40:21
ID: ss9pHX797
Sergeant, I think you found something dangerous.

327: **Sergeant Kansai**: 01/15/2011 (Sat) 14:40:27
ID: H7cKvHk1c
I might be in trouble.

328: Anonymous: 01/15/2011 (Sat) 14:40:54
ID: m9iV66g6Z
What's going on?!

329: Anonymous: 01/15/2011 (Sat) 14:40:56
ID: gBbp5D2vd
What's happening, Sergeant?

330: Anonymous: 01/15/2011 (Sat) 14:41:12
ID: nHp7s7K3u
Are you okay?

360: Anonymous: 01/15/2011 (Sat) 15:05:51
ID: fJf96cCp4
Sergeant! Is everything all right?

391: Anonymous: 01/15/2011 (Sat) 15:51:19
ID: ss9pHX797
No comment after this long must mean...

400: Anonymous: 01/15/2011 (Sat) 16:02:44
ID: ai4JjEzsg
He's trolling us.

405: Anonymous: 01/15/2011 (Sat) 16:10:01
ID: nHp7s7K3u
Please... Please say he's trolling us...

408: Anonymous: 01/15/2011 (Sat) 16:14:22
ID: fJf96cCp4
Anyone living in the area, get some people and go help him!

410: Anonymous: 01/15/2011 (Sat) 16:17:15
ID: cxjbz6cDa
Should we call the police?

412: Anonymous: 01/15/2011 (Sat) 16:19:22
ID: gBbp5D2vd
>>410
He's trespassing.
And he might be trolling us.

430: Anonymous: 01/15/2011 (Sat) 17:01:03
ID: gBbp5D2vd
Do you think the Sergeant is gone for good?

431: Anonymous: 01/15/2011 (Sat) 17:05:38
ID: nHp7s7K3u
I was just looking back through the thread. What's up with Aylg8wLma?
They told him where to go, how to get inside the house, and mentioned places with weird stuff before the Sergeant found them. Who are they?

432: Anonymous: 01/15/2011 (Sat) 17:09:01
ID: ss9pHX797
>>431
Yeah, something's fishy.

433: Anonymous: 01/15/2011 (Sat) 17:12:35
ID: ykYxw3t8q
What do you know, Aylg8wLma?

452: **Sergeant Kansai**: 01/15/2011 (Sat) 19:25:09
ID: H7cKvHk1c
Broken link

453: Anonymous: 01/15/2011 (Sat) 19:29:11
ID: fJf96cCp4
Sergeant!
What is this?

454: Anonymous: 01/15/2011 (Sat) 19:32:59
ID: utv7Nm6Ju
Sergeant, you're safe!

455: Anonymous: 01/15/2011 (Sat) 19:34:03
ID: gBbp5D2vd
So you were trolling us after all.

456: Anonymous: 01/15/2011 (Sat) 19:34:17
ID: ss9pHX797

I'm glad you're safe, but what's with the picture?
Is this one of the talismans?

457: Anonymous: 01/15/2011 (Sat) 19:36:59
ID: 5eiCbzfkm
It's really creepy.

458: Anonymous: 01/15/2011 (Sat) 19:38:22
ID: hHAx8jbj6
What is this, Sergeant?

459: Anonymous: 01/15/2011 (Sat) 19:39:17
ID: hmCarmzd8
I've never seen a talisman like that before.

460: Anonymous: 01/15/2011 (Sat) 19:40:58
ID: 4irA42jzo
Where did the Sergeant take that picture? I thought there weren't any talismans in the house.

461: Anonymous: 01/15/2011 (Sat) 19:41:11
ID: gBbp5Dsvd
Is this some religious thing? It has a torii on it.
And what about that symbol? Is it the character 了?

******

The thread's original author (Sergeant Kansai) made no further posts, and the meaning of the picture remains a mystery. To this day, no one has come forward to say that the thread was a hoax.
User Aylg8wLma, who seemed to have prior knowledge about the house, also made no further posts, and the thread is now closed.
In a separate thread called *Save the Sergeant from Paranormal Hot Spots: Live Updates from Spooky Locations in the Kinki Region*, a group of volunteers formed an investigative team to find the Sergeant and later visited the abandoned house. They found the mat in the middle of the tatami room moved to the side, but there was nothing underneath.

What do you think about this thread that leaves so many unanswered questions?
Who knows how much of it is true, but it's fun to develop theories!

Published in May 2010
in a Certain Monthly Magazine

Short Story: *Ghost Photo*

"This story is about a ghost photo I personally saw…"

A is an experienced editor at a women's fashion magazine. When I meet her, she's wearing a sophisticated designer dress, yet it's her congenial smile that leaves the biggest impression.

"For a fashion shoot, we typically reserve a studio for a couple of days and then take all the photos at once. The tight timeline makes for a very busy schedule, especially when we're working with models."

A lot of people have to be on-site. Not just the editor, but the models, their mangers, makeup artists, stylists, brand PR representatives, sales staff, writers, photographers, and all their assistants.

The editor has to manage the photo shoot, ensuring it still aligns with their vision as they take into account the other parties' varying opinions, all while keeping the process on schedule. They never have a moment's rest.

"Ambiance is essential. I always try to create a positive atmosphere that keeps everyone in good spirits."

According to A, each person on the staff has a certain vibe, and it plays a role just as crucial as their professional skill set.

"If the photographer and makeup team jell, then anyone coming to a shoot for the first time can just relax and trust us to do our thing. B is still young for a photographer, but he excels at keeping models engaged, and I can always count on him to do a good job."

* * *

Six months ago, B came to the editorial department at A's magazine looking for work, and it wasn't long before he became a regular member of A's team.

"The cover shot alone requires hundreds of photos. We check every little detail of each pose. The more famous photographers sometimes don't respond well to detailed requests, so I prefer to hire younger, more flexible photographers who listen to me when I have a certain composition in mind, and B is perfect for situations like that."

After spending more than a week in the studio taking photos, A looks through them all and chooses which ones to use in the magazine. Even after the photographer removes the obviously unusable pictures from the mass of data, there are still several hundred delivered to the editor.

"We sift through the sea of pictures and narrow it down to a couple of patterns. We tell the photographer which pictures we want, then they retouch the images, adjust the brightness, and so on. Only after they've delivered the final photos is their work considered to be done. The editors, of course, are making drafts, ordering designs, and checking copy from our writers, so there's a lot happening all at once."

One day, A couldn't decide on which image to use for a cover.

"B had taken them. I really liked a certain pose, but all of the ten or so photos he'd delivered with that pose were just the tiniest bit off. In every shot, a little strand of hair was covering the earrings our client had lent us for the ad, and sales said we couldn't use any of them."

Unwilling to give up just yet, A continued comparing the files.

"All the pictures from B had file names like IMG-0001. And as I looked through the thumbnails, I noticed he hadn't delivered everything."

For example, if the pictures A liked were labeled IMG-0010 through IMG-0020, that would equate to the tenth through the twentieth shot from the photo shoot. The file names were sequential, starting with IMG-0010, then IMG-0011, then IMG-0012, and so on. So if a bundle didn't include IMG-0013, for example, then B must not have delivered that file.

"IMG-0053 was missing. If B hadn't delivered it, it meant there must have been some mistake with the shot, or it looked so bad that even retouching wouldn't help. But I really liked that pose and wanted to find a way to make it work."

A contacted the photographer and implored him to send the undelivered picture, even if it wasn't that good. She wanted to see it at least once, no matter how unusable it was.

As expected, he told her the picture hadn't turned out and she wouldn't be able to use it. Still, he found it hard to refuse a request from the editor, especially since she had so much more experience than he did. So B begrudgingly agreed to send the picture.

The image was completely black.

"I thought maybe he'd forgotten to take the lens cap off. Obviously, we couldn't use it for the cover, so I wound up having to choose a different image with a different pose."

A few months later, a new problem arose.

"We were running a special feature on accessories, and a famous overseas brand had to pull their necklaces because their country issued a sudden mandate."

The deadline was looming, and A needed to fill in the holes on the relevant pages.

"As usual, I'd hired B to take the photos. So I called him up immediately and asked him to send me all the data he had, even if it wasn't usable."

Sensing her urgency, B sent her everything.

"Once again, IMG-0053 was black. At the time, I was rushing to put together the photos for the magazine, so I didn't have any time to think about it. But in the back of my mind, I remembered the file name and the black image."

Some days later, A was at a post-shoot party for a different project that also involved B, when she suddenly thought of the photo.

"I asked him if both photos were really mistakes like he'd said. Some photographers take good-luck shots before a photo shoot, so I thought maybe it was something like that."

B chuckled, clearly a little tipsy.

"My fifty-third photo always turns out like that. I think I might be cursed."

Freed from workplace formalities, A and those sitting nearby turned giddy with curiosity.

They pressed B for details about the curse, and unable to refuse, he began to explain.

In the early stages of his career as a photographer, before he started mainly working for fashion magazines, B took whatever odd jobs he could to get by.

One of those projects entailed a photo shoot for a regional travel magazine.

Some years before, the Ministry of Land, Infrastructure, Transport, and Tourism issued something called a Dam Card for every dam in Japan. Each card contained information on that dam and could only be obtained by visiting the location in person. Though initially popular only among a small community of enthusiasts, these cards soon caught the attention of the general public, and special tours began to fill up with people looking to collect them.

B was hired by a leisure magazine to take photos promoting tours of a certain dam.

Constructed during the mid-1950s in ●●●●●, the towering concrete wall was typical of the numerous gravity dams scattered throughout Japan. No particular feature set it apart visually, and it was mostly famous as a place where people jumped to their death.

That morning, B, the editor, and the writer rented a car and drove up to the site, then began capturing the scenery around the dam and the lake. After that, an administrator for the dam took them on a mock tour.

First, they walked along the top of the dam's massive concrete wall while the administrator described the structure and how it worked. As the writer scribbled notes, B took photos of the grounds and surrounding scenery.

Next, they moved into the inspection gallery, an area only accessible to the general public during the tour. They walked down a long flight of stairs along the dam's outer wall and entered a tunnel penetrating the massive structure. This tunnel was used to manage and maintain the dam, and a thick iron door was installed to keep out intruders. As B stood near the entrance, the cold air leaking out from the tunnel chilled him.

The tunnel was kept at 15 degrees Celsius year-round and was wide enough for two adults to stand side by side. The space, with its arched ceiling, seemed to stretch out infinitely before them, branching off here and there. The atmosphere was quite eerie, the darkness interrupted only by a series of weak fluorescent lights.

When the editor commented on this, the administrator flicked the light switch by the entrance, and their surroundings went pitch-black. He said the staff always carried a flashlight when they went into the tunnel, just in case. B could understand why.

Their group turned corner after corner, descending a flight of stairs to view the displacement monitoring room and the discharge gate room. B started to feel anxious. If he somehow got lost down here, he'd never find his way out.

At last, they reached the tour's last stop—the valve room.

Though staff usually controlled the valves directly from the monitoring room, this place allowed workers to operate them manually during an emergency. The room was surprisingly spacious, and valves with handles lined the walls.

The editor and the writer stood near the entrance and listened to the administrator's explanation, but B walked farther into the room in order to take pictures.

Right at the back, he found a locker hidden behind one of the valves.

The tall, narrow locker looked like the kind you could find in any office, and B assumed it contained cleaning supplies.

Its door was cracked open slightly.

Possessed by a desire to tidy up, B decided to shut it. First, though, he peeked inside on a whim.

But there weren't any cleaning supplies. Instead, a fancy porcelain doll sat at the bottom, staring up at him.

B reflexively yelped in surprise, prompting the editor and the writer to jog over.

Neither could believe what they were seeing.

At last, the writer calmed down enough to ask what the doll was doing there.

This is what the administrator said:

"It's been there since before I started. My predecessor told me it has to stay where it is, though I have no idea why."

The administrator's casual tone only unsettled B further. Soon, the administrator was back to explaining the valves, as if nothing had happened. At that point, the editor grinned at B. He probably wanted a photo of the doll to liven up their return trip.

The tactless request bothered B, but he couldn't refuse a client, so he surreptitiously snapped a picture of the doll when the administrator wasn't looking.

"It was the fifty-third photo of the session. In the car, on the way back, I checked IMG_0053, and the thing in it was completely black. I couldn't make it out at all. The editor was disappointed. And after that, every fifty-third photo I take has something black in it. It interferes with my work, and I really wish it would stop."

The makeup artist next to A shrieked in terror, but A was more curious.

"Why is it black, though? If the doll was cursed, shouldn't the photo have a ghost in it or something?"

B looked at A for a moment, then said, "Who knows? ...Anyway, that's all I have to say about it."

"I interview people from all walks of life in this job, and I can tell when someone is hiding something. I realized immediately that B wasn't telling us everything," A continued. "I thought the image was just black when I saw it. But B kept saying it was a photo of 'something black.' That caught my attention. You wouldn't describe a blank image that way. It felt like he knew there was something in the photograph, and he was trying to keep me from noticing."

The next day at work, A checked the black image B had sent her.

"It was pitch-black, and I couldn't see anything. So I started messing around with it."

A opened the photo in her image-editing program and increased the brightness to maximum.

It took her a moment to understand what she was looking at.

There was a row of white shapes at the top and bottom, and something curved that seemed to be set above and inside the bottom row.

"It was the inside of a mouth. I think it was a human mouth. It looked like someone had taken a picture of another person with their mouth wide open. The white rows at the top and bottom were teeth, with a tongue in the middle."

B had probably avoided telling her about the image because he didn't want to scare her. A never mentioned what she found to B.

* * *

"But after that, I started to have weird dreams. I couldn't really remember them when I woke up, but I knew they were nightmares. Some guy would chase me around a mountain, his mouth wide open. Maybe I'm cursed now, too."

To this day, B's submissions are missing the file marked IMG-0053.

Information from the Internet 4

Excerpt from the free online medical consultation website *Tell Me, Doctor!*

• Asker: 50s, female 11/14/2019
Sometimes letters seem to hover above the page, and I see sentences.
It's starting to worry me.
Is there anything that matches these symptoms?
It started about three months ago, and it's getting worse.
I mentioned it to my husband, but he brushed me off and said I was just imagining things. I've never had any major illnesses, and I'm very worried there's something wrong with me.
I'm not good with computers, so I apologize for any typos.

• Respondent: Ophthalmologist 11/15/2019
Visual distortions are tough, and they can interfere with your daily life.
Because there are no external symptoms, family members often don't understand. But eye problems can become serious if left unattended.
I recommend that you visit an ophthalmologist as soon as possible.
I can't make a precise determination based solely off your question, but hovering letters could be anything from tired eyes to a macular hole or a detached retina.
Considering your age, it could be age-related macular degeneration.
This can happen as you get older, as retinal bleeding or swelling causes your eyesight to deteriorate. It won't heal naturally, and if left alone, the symptoms could worsen. It's possible you could even go blind.
Regardless of the cause, periodic checkups and treatment usually reduce symptoms, so I recommend visiting a clinic soon.

→ Asker's reply 11/17/2019
Thank you for answering.
I'll go see an ophthalmologist.
But I get the feeling this might be something else. It's like the letters hover in the air and form a sentence. Like someone is trying to tell me something.
Sometimes the words appear to be written just for me. All the letters use the same blocky font.

• Respondent: Psychologist 11/18/2019
I saw your question and your reply to the other doctor.
Please don't take this the wrong way, but are you starting to forget things more frequently? Or have you experienced any traumatic events, like the loss of a close friend or family member?
People your age can often develop Alzheimer's or behavioral disorders.
As long as you know how to handle it, there's no reason to be scared.
Just to be safe, why don't you show this exchange to your family?
If it's nothing, then you can all have a good laugh about it. But I urge you to discuss this with people close to you instead of brooding over it all by yourself.

→ Asker's reply 11/18/2019
Thank you for your thoughtful response.
I wondered about that, too, since it's hard to notice the onset of dementia in yourself. I showed my husband this website.
It doesn't seem like I've been forgetting things. I prepare dinner every day as usual, so I think I'm fine.
But I can't say for certain that I'm not losing my mind.
My husband said I worry too much. But I just can't stop feeling like someone out there is trying to get me to read something.
It started with a supermarket flyer.
Some letters floated up from a block of text, forming a sentence.
Sometimes it would be newspapers or books, and the sentences would be quite long.
It happened another time when I was choosing a pen at a stationary store.
Those blocky letters were there on the test pad. I'm not sure why, but it felt like they were picking up where those other sentences left off.

After that, it happened with the waiting list at a restaurant when I went out with a friend. Then it was on the neighborhood association circular.

The sentences didn't make any sense and really disturbed me, so I didn't write them down. But they seemed to be asking me something.

Even now, those same sentences keep floating up around me, or I'll see the blocky letters on something I just happen to glance at.

When I look back at what I've written here, I can tell I sound crazy.

I haven't had any major traumas. My parents live far away, but they're doing fine.

That said, I can think of one thing that might have caused this.

I'm not too upset about it, and I don't think there's any reason to tell a doctor, so I think I'll keep it to myself.

→ Psychologist's reply 11/19/2019

Thank you for your response.

Based on your answer, this seems to be really troubling you.

Please don't doubt yourself. I recommend speaking with a psychologist at least once to help address your concerns.

Don't deny what you're feeling, and talk with a specialist about your experiences.

I'm sure they will discuss the matter with you and help you overcome your worries.

I am curious about what you think caused your symptoms, though.

Even if you believe it's nothing, it might be putting significant stress on your subconscious mind.

I suggest you discuss it along with your symptoms when you speak to a medical professional.

→ Asker's reply 11/19/2019

I followed your advice and am going with my husband to see a doctor next Saturday. The cause was something really minor, but since you kindly listened to what I said, I'll tell you what happened. It's very silly, though.

My son is in college, and three months ago, he and a group of his friends went to check out a place they'd heard was haunted. I think it was some run-down hotel or a corporate retreat somewhere in ●●●●●.

Silly, right? I warned them not to go because it was dangerous and would bother the people living nearby, but they didn't listen.
My son said the building was a mess and some parts of it were collapsed, so they didn't go too far inside. But near the entrance, they looked through the reception desk and found a notebook.
It was one of those guest logs they often have at tourist attractions. There were lots of comments from kids on school trips and from workers on company retreats, none of them all that noteworthy.
There was something odd about the notebook, though. The second half was blank, except for a weird comment on the last page.
My son and his friends didn't understand what it meant, but apparently it was some kind of request. He said it really unnerved them.
He told my husband and I about it over dinner.
I started seeing the hovering letters a little while later.
The sentences they formed were similar, and it kind of upset me.
Rationally, I know things like that aren't real. At my age, I'm ashamed to admit I even considered it.
If I mentioned it to my son, he might go out there again.
It's embarrassing, but I will tell my doctor about it. Just in case.
Thank you for listening to me.

→ Asker's reply 11/21/2019
It's me again. I think there may really be something wrong with my head.
My neighbor stopped by yesterday. She said I had placed a weird letter in her mailbox. I don't remember doing it at all.
We met each other through the PTA when my son was in elementary school, so I've known her for close to a decade, and I'm sure she's telling the truth.
She showed me the letter. It was definitely my handwriting, and the envelope had my name on it. I have the letter with me, so I'll type out what it says.

I am looking for myself.
Thank you for finding me.
I am looking at you.
Can you become me?
My adorable child.
Please raise it together with me.
It cries for more friends.

Anyone can invite someone else.
So please.
But that is not enough.
Only those who have created life understand.
Please guide everyone from a higher place.
Until then, I will be watching.

When I read the letter, I got the feeling it said the same things as the hovering letters I've been seeing.
My husband and neighbors are all worried.
I didn't mention this before, but I sometimes hear a voice as if it's coming from right beside my ear.
I checked online, and I think it might be something like schizophrenia.
If I go see a doctor, do you think I should see someone in psychosomatic medicine?
I will ask my husband to take a day off tomorrow and drive me to a clinic.

Published in July 2018
in a Certain Monthly Magazine

Short Story:
Cheating

"My hair has finally grown out."

A stroked the lengthy strands, dyed light brown and grown long enough to run down her back.

She'd last cut her hair after she and her ex-boyfriend split up. I asked her if it was a symbolic way to break with her past, but she shook her head.

"No, I'm not that type of person. I actually didn't want to cut it."

And with that, she started telling me her story.

About two years ago, A was in her third year of university and dating a guy she'd met in her school's tennis club.

They had been together since their first year and got along well. Sometimes, they'd even go on trips with friends from the club.

"We'd party all night long almost every day back then. We were pretty wild."

One day, A was spending a typical night drinking at a friend's house.

"It was me, my boyfriend, and two other people. We were all super drunk, and somebody suggested we tell scary stories."

They took turns sharing the typical sort of spooky tales everyone's heard from somewhere or other. Helped along by the alcohol, everyone got really into it.

But after a few rounds, they had exhausted their cache and moved on to the subject of *Kokkuri-san*, a game where someone writes down all fifty phonetic *kana* on a slip of paper and uses it like a Ouija board.

"We all reminisced about gathering after class in elementary school and playing the game. Apparently, some regions in Japan call it by a different name. My boyfriend's hometown calls it *Cupid-san*, but it's essentially the same thing."

Since the group was discussing it, someone proposed trying it out. But it would require a paper with all fifty *kana*, and no one was sober enough to write them all out. The inebriated group's enthusiasm started to wane.

"One of my friends noticed the change in mood and decided to tell another story. This one was about a game that had been popular at an elementary school they briefly attended as a kid. It was easy to do and didn't require any preparation."

Their parents had moved frequently for work, so they'd changed schools often. When they were in third and fourth grade, they'd attended a school in ●●●●●, and the game had been popular there.

"It was called *Mashiro-sama*, and it's really easy. You just stand up, raise both hands above your head, then repeat '*Mashiro-sama*, *Mashiro-sama*, come on over' while jumping in place three times. That's it. When you're done, *Mashiro-sama* will supposedly tell you your future."

But if Ouija boards, for example, communicate by moving the planchette, how do you receive *Mashiro-sama's* message?

"I asked my friend, but they said they didn't know. The whole thing was really vague. But apparently, some of the kids at their school loved the game."

But at the time, A's group was bored and looking for something to do, so they weren't that worried about the details.

"My boyfriend volunteered first. He staggered up, swaying as he jumped. He said, '*Mashiro-sama*, *Mashiro-sama*, come on over.' He looked so funny that we all burst out laughing. Seeing that, he handed me his phone and asked me to record him doing it again so he could post it on social media.

After taking the video, I handed him back his phone, and he immediately uploaded it."

A watched her boyfriend blankly as he fiddled with his phone. Then, all of a sudden, he gasped.

"Someone liked the video less than five seconds after I uploaded it. I don't even know the account."

A checked her boyfriend's screen and saw a single account name in the list of likes.

"They used the default avatar, the one that just looks like a silhouette. The space for their name was blank, and the username was a random jumble of meaningless numbers."

The account contained no posts, had zero followers, and was only following her boyfriend.

A found this creepy, but her boyfriend seemed unfazed.

Naturally, *Mashiro-sama* delivered no prophecy, so the group moved on to the next topic. Eventually, the party came to an end, and they headed home.

"It all started after that. The weird account would like everything my boyfriend posted, no matter what. For example, he'd post a picture of me when we were out on a date. I care about how I look in pictures, so I'd check his wall from my phone, and that account would have already liked it, even though he'd just posted it. That's creepy, right? I told him to block the person several times, but he seemed to enjoy getting the free likes and didn't see any problem with it..."

The account didn't seem to prefer any specific kind of picture or video—it simply liked every single post her boyfriend made.

A secretly began to suspect something was happening behind her back.

"I thought he might be cheating on me, and that the woman was using a throwaway account to stalk him. She probably figured liking all his posts would put pressure on our relationship, since we both checked his account. I assumed he knew and that was why he wouldn't block her."

About a month later, A's suspicions intensified.

"My boyfriend became a little distant. He didn't seem to enjoy our time together as much, and I began to feel like he wasn't there in the moment with me anymore. I asked him if I'd done something to upset him, but he denied it. It made me sad to think he might not be interested in me anymore."

One night, A stayed over at her boyfriend's house.

He was distant that night, too, so they turned on the TV for background noise to hide the awkwardness, then fiddled with their phones before going to bed early.

Late that night, A woke up to the mattress squeaking.

"I realized my boyfriend had gotten up and left the bed. I was half conscious and figured he'd just gone to the bathroom, so I went back to sleep."

The next time she woke up, his side of the bed was still empty.

"I checked my phone, and it was three in the morning. I didn't know when he'd gotten out of bed, but it felt like a fair amount of time had passed."

She wondered where he could be and debated going to look for him. Then a faint voice reached her from the hallway.

"I heard this low muttering. It sounded like he was talking with somebody."

A sneaked out of bed and peered into the hall.

"I slowly cracked open the door and looked out, but the hall was dark. I could see a sliver of light coming from the bathroom, though. My boyfriend was inside, talking."

Her boyfriend had gotten up in the middle of the night to spend a considerable amount of time talking in the bathroom. He had to be on the phone. Already suspicious, A decided to find out who he was talking to.

She crept down the dark hallway and pressed her ear against the bathroom door.

"He kept apologizing. Stuff like 'I'm sorry,' 'I can't do that,' and 'Please forgive me.' I assumed he'd gotten involved with some horrible woman who was trying to make him break up with me."

* * *

Hearing his pitiful voice, she felt her feelings for him chill.

“I figured, whatever. There’s no point in dating a guy like that. But at the same time, I was really mad. If we were going to split up, I wanted proof he was cheating, so I could confront him and break things off myself.”

A returned to bed, but her boyfriend stayed in the bathroom all night. That morning, she left his apartment like nothing had happened.

Exactly one week later, A went over to his place again to spend the night.

“I was on a mission. I was determined to find proof that he was cheating.”

She figured his phone would provide the best evidence. Thankfully, she had accidentally seen him enter his password while they were out one time, and she still remembered it.

After they went to bed that night, A waited until her boyfriend had started snoring before snatching his phone and sneaking out of bed.

“I didn’t want to be in the same room if she happened to call him, so I went to the bathroom, just like he had the time before.”

Slinking down the dark hallway, she crept into the bathroom and unlocked his phone.

First, she opened the messenger app and checked the names. But she only found wholly normal exchanges with their mutual friends from the club.

She was sure the name of whoever he’d been talking to would be in his call history, at least. But she couldn’t find any record of a call at that time of night. She checked his other applications that included chat functions but found nothing.

“If he’d deleted his call history, then he was definitely up to no good. No one goes to the bathroom in the middle of the night to talk to themselves. So I kept digging.”

His photos folder didn’t produce anything, either. She’d just about given up, when something occurred to her.

What about the account that had been liking his social media posts?

They might be communicating through the app’s messenger function. She launched the program and checked his DMs.

* * *

"That was when I found it. He'd been exchanging DMs with that account. But it wasn't what I'd expected."

The screen displayed a long list of messages from her boyfriend.

I'm sorry.
I'm sorry.
I'm sorry.
I'm sorry.
I'm sorry.
I'm sorry.
I'm sorry.
I'm sorry.
I'm sorry.
I'm sorry.
I'm sorry.
I'm sorry.

"There wasn't a single response from the other person, just him sending 'I'm sorry' over and over. There were so many messages that I couldn't check them all. It must have been several weeks' worth. It seemed like he was sending dozens every day."

A found this extremely bizarre. She gave up on finding evidence he'd cheated and decided to just ask him about it directly.

Still holding his phone, she opened the bathroom door and found her boyfriend standing in the middle of the dark hallway.

"It was too dark to see his face, but I could tell something was off. He didn't say anything. He just stood there watching me. We looked at each other in silence for about thirty seconds. Then he lurched forward and grabbed my arm."

She reflexively apologized, scared that her boyfriend might lash out in anger. But he just wordlessly yanked her by the arm into the living room.

"He would get carried away sometimes, but he'd never been violent. I was absolutely terrified. I begged him to let me go, but he wouldn't."

Fearing that he might start hitting her, A struggled wildly, trying to wrest her arm free.

At last, she thought he had let go. But then he abruptly shoved her away.

A fell, hitting her head on the corner of a low table. She stayed there for a while, unable to move.

"I was dazed. I just laid there on the floor, watching him walk back down the hall."

He returned to the living room holding a pair of scissors.

That was when she saw his face clearly for the first time.

She said he was smiling really wide but crying at the same time. A stared hazily at his tear-streaked grin.

He approached A, took a handful of her long hair, and cut it clean off with the scissors.

"I couldn't hear him all that well, but he kept muttering weird things, like 'This will do for now' and 'The doll will replace you.'"

Still holding her hair, he walked over to the bed and picked up a stuffed animal.

They had won it from an arcade claw machine on a date, back when times were better.

He feverishly wrapped her hair around it.

Then he walked past A and left the apartment, still clutching the hair-wrapped stuffed animal.

"That was it. As soon as I could move again, I left. I never saw him again after that, and I don't want to. I went to the hospital, and they told me I'd only suffered a slight concussion, nothing more. But he had chopped off my hair… I went to a hair salon to have them even it up, but it wound up much shorter than I like."

When she told the other club members what had happened, they could hardly believe it, and they were deeply angry.

Some people wanted to confront A's boyfriend on her behalf, but he stopped showing up to club events. He even stopped going to school and vacated his apartment.

* * *

"At first, I was shocked, sad, and upset. My feelings were all over the place. But now that I can think back on it with a calmer mind, I realize how strange it all was."

Then A seemed to mutter something to herself.

"But what was he cheating on me with? And what was he apologizing to?"

About a Place in the Kinki Region 4

"I've come this far. I think it's time to visit ●●●●● for myself."

That was what Ozawa told me.
Of course, I tried to stop him.
But he went anyway.

This is where *About a Place in the Kinki Region* ends.
I'm trying to find Ozawa.
Please contact me if you have any information that could help.

Scary School
Stories Series

Excerpt from *Scary School Stories,* Vol. 2, "Chapter 1: Seven School Mysteries" (first published in 2003):

• The School with Nine Mysteries

Most schools are said to have seven mysteries, but there's one elementary school that has nine. What follows is a brief description of each.

#1: The Stairwell Mirror

A large mirror hangs on the wall of one of the landings in the stairwell used by the fourth, fifth, and sixth graders. The ghost of a former principal appears there and drags children who don't listen to their teachers into the mirror.

#2: The Dancing Dummy

The anatomical model in the third-floor science room dances every night. A long time ago, a teacher assigned to patrol the school after dark was doing their rounds when they heard a noise coming from the science room, which was locked. They peeked in through the hallway window and saw the anatomical model dancing giddily.

#3: *Mashiro-san*

Anyone staying at school until very late might run into a terrifying ghost called *Mashiro-san*. No one knows what *Mashiro-san* looks like because everyone who encounters it dies.

* * *

#4: The White Hand in the Pool

Long ago, a girl drowned in the deep pool used by the older students and turned into a ghost that pulls kids under. Her white hand reached out and grabbed the leg of a student who used the pool during summer break without permission.

#5: The Self-Playing Piano

The piano in the back of the gym used for recitals will sometimes start playing all by itself. In the past, a student was supposed to play the school's anthem at her year's graduation ceremony, but no matter how much she tried, she couldn't play it right. She was so troubled that she killed herself, and her ghost is still practicing.

#6: The Painting of a Woman

There's a painting of a woman in the art storage room, and no one knows who made it. Anyone who looks at the painting will start seeing the woman in their dreams. That's why the art storage room is locked, and no one ever goes inside.

#7: The Floating Head in the Covered Passage

A floating head wanders the grounds at night. Once, a kid forgot his homework and went back to school very late. When he was walking along the covered passage between two buildings, a floating head with a huge smile flew toward him really fast.

#8: The End-of-Day Bell

The announcement room's automated bell sometimes plays three minutes after five o'clock, instead of right on the hour. That's the same time a student committed suicide a long time ago. Anyone who hears that bell will feel like they want to die, too.

#9: Akio

The ghost of a boy named Akio haunts the school. He hides in dark places, like in the shadow of the blackout curtain in the multipurpose room, or in the last stall in the bathroom, asking people if they want to be his friend. You have to say no, because if you become his friend, he'll eat you.

******

Excerpt from *Scary School Stories*, Vol. 6, "Chapter 3: Scary Stories from Around the School" (first published 2007):

• The Jumping Woman

This is the story of T, a fourth grader.

T was in his room on the second floor, doing homework after dinner.

He glanced outside his window and saw the face of an incredibly scary woman appearing and disappearing.

The woman was jumping two stories into the air to peer through his window.

T screamed and ran to tell his mother what he'd seen. He found his mother standing at the bottom of the stairs.

But just as he started to speak to her, he saw her staring up at him.

It was the woman, wearing his mother's clothes.

T and his entire family have been missing ever since.

• Akito and the Phone Booth

Near R's elementary school is an old phone booth that no one ever uses.

If you walk inside at five in the evening and pick up the handset, you can talk to a boy named Akito. Rumor has it that Akito will grant any wish you ask for.

R wanted to get to know a boy she liked in her class, so she went to the phone booth one evening and picked up the handset.

She waited for a while, but she didn't hear anything. Disappointed, she said her wish anyway.

When she left the phone booth, she saw a boy in shorts and a T-shirt, even though it was the middle of winter.

R asked if he was Akito, and he opened his huge mouth.

No one has seen R since.

An E-mail from K

Hi. This is K.

Thank you for all your help the other day.
Have things settled down any?
I'm sorry to hear about the new guy.
Please take good care of yourself.

I'm not sure it's appropriate to bring this up right now, considering the situation, but I have an update on the things you asked me about at our meeting.

It's about S, the chief editor.

After we spoke, I checked the data S sent us when he quit.
I found some things involving ●●●●● and have included them here.
He was also looking into ●●●●●. Or rather, he found out about ●●●●● while researching something else.
You'll see once you read what I sent you.

The date on the folder with these files was from just before he quit, so this must have been his last job. I have no idea how he planned to turn it into a story, though.

* * *

I wanted to know more about S, so I asked someone from HR who still works there and who was hired around the same time as I was.

They said it was probably all right to tell me now, since it's been so long. It turns out S quit because of his wife.

According to the rumor mill, she suddenly developed a mental illness, and he quit to look after her.

She was apparently in really bad shape, making strange calls to his work and sending weird letters.

The editorial department is used to strange people contacting us, so I didn't realize that some of the letters had come from S's wife. But it sounds like it was an open secret among the part-timers in the administration office.

I know we butted heads, but I wish he would've talked to me about it, since we were in the same department.

Maybe I could have done something. But it's too late now.

No one knows where he is, not even my friend in HR.

They said he looked deeply troubled when he announced his resignation, and it didn't feel right to ask him about his future plans.

When I heard that, it reminded me of you and the newbie.

I decided to go ahead and send you the information, but to be honest, I'm really concerned.

We're just writers providing entertainment; we're not detectives. So please don't get in over your head.

You'll have to excuse me for sending this via e-mail, but my phone call wouldn't connect for some reason.

Please call me back once you've read this.

Take care.

Published in October 2012
in a Certain Monthly Magazine

Short Story: *What He Saw*

Excerpt from S's files—*About the Stone 1*:

"This is about something my friend saw."
That was the first thing A said.

A goes to a university in the Kansai region.

His school is a famous private institution, and students come from all over Japan to attend, but A was one of the locals.

With good grades in high school and no desire to move to Tokyo, he followed the same path as many of his friends and chose the well-regarded local university. Though it was close enough for him to commute from his parents' house, A moved out with a little financial help from his folks, relishing the chance to live on his own for the first time.

"The kids who come from far away all study really hard. But I just went to college because it's what you're supposed to do after high school, so I wasn't really like them. That's why I wound up hanging out with other people from Kansai."

A spent lots of time with two other local kids. We'll call them B and C.

"B and I had a bunch of the same classes, and we often ended up eating lunch together. Our conversations weren't deep or anything. B was just a really outgoing guy. Our major was full of introverts, so we kind of became friends by default. One day, B showed up with a girl. That was C. He said she was a friend from his club, but I could tell right away that they would end up dating."

They all started talking, and A found C to be an endearing person who laughed easily. She and A hit it off, and before long, the three of them had formed a tight-knit group.

Then, last year during the summer, something happened. The trio had skipped their afternoon classes and were chatting in the cafeteria when B made a suggestion.

"He asked if we wanted to go see a pretty night view that evening. B lived with his parents, and they let him use the family car. He had just gotten his driver's license and wanted us to tag along for some driving practice."

B suggested a spot well known among locals.

An hour's drive from the university, on the side of a mountain pass, there was a little clearing. It didn't have a viewing deck or anything like that, and it had never appeared in any magazine. But it boasted nice, panoramic views of the city, and it was a popular spot among couples and driving enthusiasts looking to take a break.

"C and I were up for it, but I had work that afternoon. So we went our separate ways, and B came to pick me up later."

When A, who worked at a restaurant, finished up and stepped outside, he found a small, boxy kei car waiting. B sat in the driver's seat, beaming at him through the window. C waved in A from her spot in the back. He climbed inside, and the car drove off. It was almost midnight.

"None of us needed to attend our morning classes the next day, and we chatted excitedly the whole drive. We put in a CD B had borrowed from someone and cranked up the volume, then we all sang along."

They arrived a little after one AM. It was a weeknight, and the overlook was deserted.

After parking the car in the clearing, they took selfies in front of the distant city lights. In between, they would lean against the fence, chatting about nothing in particular and just enjoying the break from their typical routine.

"At first, all three of us were talking, but after I went back to the car to get a cigarette, I noticed the two of them making eyes at each other. I was kind of put out, but I know when to give people space, so I hung back and took a smoke break by the car."

A little irritated, A watched his friends' silhouettes against the city lights.

B began to lean closer to C, but just as their shoulders were about to touch, C suddenly looked away and started pointing. It seemed she'd noticed something.

"She was gesturing toward the edge of the clearing. B turned and seemed to notice it, too. I could hear them talking about something."

The little clearing had a small parking area and a space to enjoy the view. At the edge, there was also a spot to sit and rest.

"It was kind of like a little gazebo. It had a roof and four benches set up in a square. That was what C was pointing at. I figured they were going to make out over there while I was gone."

Just as A suspected, B and C began to move toward the gazebo. Annoyed, he clicked his tongue at their shadows, then lit another cigarette and gazed down at his phone.

"I messed around on my phone for a while, but then I heard someone yell, and I looked up to see them both bolting toward me. They were practically in tears."

A glanced over at the gazebo. Squinting into the darkness, he saw something strange.

But before he had the chance to say anything, B yelled for him to get in the car. B and C practically shoved him into the back seat, then C climbed in next to him, and the car sped away.

Just as they exited the clearing, A started to say something about what he'd seen. But C yelled at him to stop.

"Shut up! Don't say anything."

A had never heard C shout like that, and he fell into silent confusion.

In the driver's seat, B looked deeply troubled.

* * *

The car tore down the mountain road. As a strange silence spread through the vehicle, they started to hear something.

"It came from outside the car. Weird voices that might have been screaming or laughing. We kept hearing them from the woods on both sides of the road. It was like they were following us."

There were multiple voices, loud enough for the car's occupants to hear them clearly through the closed doors. It sounded like a huge group of people, all shouting in different voices.

"Ahhhh! Ahhhh!"

"Hee-hee-hee-hee!"

"Ah-ha-ha-ha-ha-ha-ha-ha!"

"Hee-ha-ha! Hee-ha-ha!"

At first, A thought they might be animal sounds, but he was quickly proved wrong by the sheer variation. He could almost see them—men and women of all ages screaming at random.

A was terrified as C muttered beside him.

"They found us. What do we do?"

At that, B exploded.

"What is all this?! These voices! And those people!"

Wondering what B meant, A started to speak. But C gave him a look, and he closed his mouth. Then she turned to B.

"Did you see something, B?"

Gripping the wheel tightly, B sounded irritated.

"What do you mean? You saw it, too, C! We went over there because you said you saw something! There were a bunch of people around some weird rock up on a stage. They were all jumping and talking."

* * *

The voices outside seemed to grow louder.
C desperately pressed him to elaborate.

"Talking? What were they saying?"

B sounded perplexed. "You heard it, too, C. It sounded like a chant. Like 'Ruki emu…'"

B began repeating what he'd heard, then suddenly stopped.
C urged him to continue, but he didn't answer.
A looked at the rear-view mirror and saw B, expressionless, his mouth shut tight.
He was just gripping the wheel, as though he'd forgotten all the fear and panic of a few moments earlier.
The random voices outside continued. The loud chanting sounded like it was coming from right next to the car.
B suddenly pressed the play button on the car stereo, resuming the pop song they'd been listening to on the way there. He hadn't touched the volume, so the music blasted from the speakers.
The voices outside mixed with the music, turning the car into a cacophonous hell.
A twisted to face C, trying to understand what was going on. She looked tense.
Suddenly, B shouted.

"Everyone, listen up. We're gonna pass through this together! Yeah! Hey, hey, hey!"

A jumped at the unexpected declaration.
"After that, B started shouting some sort of chant or sutra. He was so loud that his voice drowned out everything else. He just kept going. I couldn't make it out from the back seat, but it sounded like he was chanting along to something rather than repeating something he'd memorized. That's when I realized he was hearing something other than the pop music."

Unable to stand it anymore, C started crying. A panicked.

As B continued to chant, A grabbed his arm and yelled at him. But his words were drowned out by the noise.

He shook B's arm, causing the car to swerve.

Just as he bent forward, bracing himself, the car screeched to a halt.

Terrified, A peeked out the window. The car was stopped diagonally across the mountain road, half its body in the opposite lane.

Just then, A noticed the voices from the forest, the music inside the car, and B's voice had all gone quiet.

Then, seemingly back to normal, B started the car.

Silence reigned both inside and outside the vehicle, as though the previous commotion had been a collective dream.

A asked B what he'd been doing.

"Oh, I felt a kind of weird just now," he said casually. "Sorry about that."

"We made it home safely that night. But starting the next day, B began to act a little strange. His personality didn't go through any drastic changes, but whenever we'd hang out, something felt off. He would speak to me normally, then suddenly go blank. It was like a part of him was somewhere else."

At some point, B quit his club and began devoting all his time to a bizarre spiritual organization in town. After a while, he stopped coming to school almost completely. B had never acted like that before. He urged A and C to join his new group, but they refused. The whole thing sounded creepy to them.

The two gradually distanced themselves from B.

"I think it all started with what we saw that night. C has something of a sixth sense, so when she heard the voices outside the car, she decided we should pretend not to have seen anything. She thought that might help us escape. I'm glad I didn't say anything. I saw something, too, but not what B described. It was far away and it was at night, so it was only a vague shape in the darkness. But it wasn't a stone."

If A didn't see a stone, then what did he see? When I asked, he just shook his head.

"I'd prefer not to say. I don't want to draw their attention by talking about it. C might have seen something different, but we try to never mention it. This story is only about my friend seeing something strange and then becoming strange himself. C and I just happened to be there. That's our story, and we're sticking to it."

Sharing this secret strengthened the pair's bond.

A short while later, C confessed her feelings for A.

They're now dating.

About a Place in the Kinki Region

4

"I've come this far. I think it's time to visit ●●●●● for myself."

That was what Ozawa told me.
Of course, I tried to stop him.
But he went anyway.

Two months later, he was dead.
They found him in ●●●●●.

Dear readers, I'm so sorry for deceiving you.
This is where *About a Place in the Kinki Region* ends.

Letters to the Editor 3

• The First Letter

Dear XXX,

It's been a while.
This is OOOOO.
Do you remember me?

I found your business card when I was cleaning out a drawer, so I decided to write to you.
I have something I want to say to you.

You humiliated me and my child.
I don't even want to remember it.
But I won't let you say you've forgotten.
It's all your fault. You and all the other reporters.

You approached us looking sympathetic.
And I endured, because I knew it was a test to lead me to a higher place.
But that doesn't mean you will be absolved of your sins.

You should atone.
Come and listen to my story one more time.

This time, though, you must spread everything I say, exactly as I say it.

I will not say anything here.
You lower-level people wouldn't understand, even if I wrote it all down.
I saved that child.
If you would get the word out, I know some people would understand.
Because something as marvelous as this rarely ever happens.

Anyway, contact me.
Make sure you do.
I'm waiting.

******

• The Second Letter

XXX,

Why haven't you contacted me
You should confess your sins.

I will give you a little more time.
Make sure you contact me

******

• The Third Letter

XXX,

This is my final letter.

Contact me

******

• The Fourth Letter

Dear XXX,

Hello.
I have not received any word from you.

Well, that doesn't matter now.
I am going to a higher place.

I will open your chakra.
We must remember to be grateful.
Thank you for finding me.

**At the end of the letter is a handwritten note, presumably from an editor in another department. It reads:*

"O, these letters came from that crazy lady in the ●●●●● case we reported on earlier. They sounded a little spooky, so I thought you might want them for your magazine. Ha-ha."

Published in December 2014
in a Certain Monthly Magazine

Short Story:
Karaoke

Excerpt from S's files—*About the Stone 2*:

A, a businessman in Nagasaki, experienced something peculiar at a high school reunion over the summer Obon holiday.

Three years had passed since A entered the workforce. He'd stayed in his hometown, but many of his friends had left. As time went by, they contacted one another less frequently, so the reunion was a good opportunity to catch up with old friends.

"I knew it'd be a big event. In the span of just three years, some people had already gotten married or were working themselves ragged in Tokyo. I was pretty much the same as always, but everyone else seemed really different. I felt a little awkward at first, but as we kept talking, I realized no one had really changed at heart. It was nice."

A and the others had rented out a bar for the official party. When that was over, about half the group headed to a darts bar for another round. Now thoroughly drunk, they started to feel like they were back in high school. Spirits were high.

"By the time we left, it was after midnight. Some people took taxis home, but me and three of my good friends resolved to keep drinking until dawn. Since all the bars were closed, we went to a twenty-four-hour karaoke place."

They ended up at a chain in Nagasaki City.

The person at the front desk looked annoyed with the drunkards but gave them a room all the same. After pouring into the booth, they started singing.

"We were all totally wasted. We sang anime songs and laughed until we cried. It was fantastic."

However, the excitement didn't last long. By three AM, A's friends started to fade and fall asleep on the table.

"The other guys all lived in Tokyo, and the long trip must've tired them out. I was the only one still awake."

Not in the mood to sing songs by himself, A scrolled through his phone. But sleep eventually overtook him, too.

"I don't remember it, but I caught myself nodding off and realized I'd been sleeping."

He woke to find the other three still passed out. Groggy from drinking, A was checking the schedule for the first train that morning when he realized there was something strange about the room.

"It had gone completely silent. Even when you don't have a song queued up, the TV is still playing music videos or interviews for whatever singers the labels are promoting. And that's exactly what was on when I fell asleep. But when I woke up, the room was totally quiet."

A turned to the screen and saw a peculiar image.

"It was weirdly pixelated, like a home movie from a few decades ago. There were lots of people just standing around silently."

There in the dark room, he stared at the image, captivated.

It looked like a group photo. There were about ten people standing in a line in front of a forest, with a strange object right in the center. There were both men and women, elderly folks and children not yet in school. Each person dressed differently: Some were in suits, while others wore farm clothes. They represented a wide range of ages and appearances, but all of them stared at A with blank, emotionless faces.

In the center of the image was a platform, about as high as an adult's hips, supporting a large stone set atop a cushion.

* * *

"On our school trip to Osaka, some friends and I took a picture around the Billiken statue. The image reminded me of that. It looked like a commemorative photo taken at some tourist attraction. But no one seemed to be enjoying themselves."

None of the people moved, so at first A assumed the screen was showing a still image. But as he watched, he noticed the tree branches and leaves in the background swaying.

"I thought it was a preview for a horror movie or something, but it was pretty avant-garde for a trailer. I watched for a couple of minutes, but absolutely no one said anything."

But just as A started to lose interest, someone in the image spoke.

"Please pass through."

The words weren't what surprised A, though. It was what the other people did.

"The ones not speaking opened their mouths really wide, like some kind of signal. But their facial expressions never changed."

Then another person spoke.

"Please come here."

The whole time, the others kept their mouths opened wide.

Then another person spoke. This time it was a young child.

"You need to do it."

It felt like when a whole class gives a shared speech at their graduation, each person standing up to contribute a few rehearsed lines.

"I don't have a sixth sense, but I broke out in goose bumps. I knew something was wrong."

He ran to the TV and turned down the volume. He tried to switch off the screen, but he was too panicked to find the button.

* * *

"I knew I had to do something, so I picked up the room's phone and called the front desk."

It rang for a while, but no one answered. As he waited, A found his eyes drawn to the video against his will. He couldn't hear it anymore, but the people were still taking turns speaking.

More than ten rings later, someone finally picked up.

"Please come quickly."

The voice on the other end belonged to an elderly man.

At that moment, someone fitting that description was speaking on the television screen. The words coming through the phone perfectly matched the movements of his mouth.

A hurried out of the room.

"I'm not sure why I did that. I think I just wanted out of there."

But as soon as he got into the hall, he froze.

The doors lining both sides of the passage were all half open, and people were leaning out, watching him with blank expressions.

"Men, women, children, older people. They were all staring like they'd been waiting for me to leave the room."

A stood rooted to the spot as all of them began to open their mouths wide.

That's when he dashed back inside the room.

"I woke up everyone, half-mad, almost in tears. But by then, the screen was showing the regular feed of videos again. Everyone was really worried about me because I was in such a panic."

One of A's friends called the front desk again. An irritated staff member picked up and asked if something had broken.

"There was still some time before the first train, but I told everyone we needed to get out of there."

The four of them left and walked down a quiet street lined with bars, under a hazy, predawn sky. A related every last detail of what had happened.

Just as he finished, everyone's phone rang.

"All the calls came from the same number. Isn't that strange? How can one number call four different phones at the same time? And it was just past four in the morning."

No one answered. Their phones rang for a long time.

"Later, I went through my call log and checked the number online. It matched one from an abandoned retirement home in the Kanto region. The place had been on the news a while back because of a mass suicide. If that was really where the calls came from, I'm glad none of us picked up."

About a Place in the Kinki Region

4

My last meeting with Ozawa was at that same café in Jinbocho.

We sat down and waited for our drinks. Once they'd arrived, he mixed liquid sweetener into his iced caffe latte and started talking.

"Will you listen to my theory?"

I decided to hear him out. The following is what he told me.

******

Earlier, we both agreed that the mountain caller is obsessed with women and women only. We learned from *The Truth Behind the Mass-Hysteria Incident at the School Camping Trip* and *New UMA Discovered! The White Man!* that the mountain caller itself doesn't leave the mountain. Instead, it gains control over men and uses them to lure women to the mountain. We don't know if those men are still alive or if they're all dead...

I'd suspected for some time that the purpose of inviting women—especially young women—was to make them "brides." Though I'm not sure if this thing has the same concept of the word as we do.

Maybe the mountain caller influences both the men it uses and the women it lures to toss their "bodies" over the side of the dam.

That could explain why the dam is such an infamous suicide spot...

If that's true, the girl from *A True Story! New Developments Regarding a Missing Girl in Nara?* might be somewhere at the bottom of the dam, her body still undiscovered.

But, as we saw in *Cheating*, a person can offer a doll in lieu of a woman, sparing her from becoming a bride. A few people even managed to survive without offering any sacrifices, like in *New UMA Discovered! The White Man!* and *Waiting*.

I assume the *Masshiro-san* and *Mashiro-sama* games the elementary schoolers talked about must have originated from kids living in the apartment complex within the mountain caller's domain. Because it's huge, white, and humanoid, they called it *Masshiro-san* or *Mashiro-sama*, which both mean Mister White. And the game seems to have involved offering some kind of sacrifice, just like in *Cheating*.

******

Ozawa, having talked nonstop up to this point, paused to catch his breath. Then he continued.

"I'm close. I can feel it. There's still a lot of unknowns, including the red woman and the sticker, but I feel like I can just about connect everything together. This special edition is going to be spectacular."

He sounded excited.

"I've come this far. I think it's time to visit ●●●●● for myself."

That was what Ozawa told me.

Of course, I tried to stop him.

But he went anyway.

* * *

Two months later, he was dead.
They found him in ●●●●●.

Dear readers, I'm so sorry for deceiving you.
This is where *About a Place in the Kinki Region* ends.

Transcript of an Interview 3

Yes, yes, hello. Nice to meet you.

Well… I guess I'll have an Earl Grey tea. Hot.

So you never met O?

I heard. You used to work with O's old coworker, right? K, was it?

O called me one day out of the blue. He said a former colleague told him about a writer investigating ●●●●●, and asked if I would let you interview me, since the two of us did some research on the place a long time ago. I said yes because I can't figure out what to do for my next book and thought that maybe talking with you would give me some ideas.

So you're a freelance writer, huh? Times are tough for us, aren't they? All the publishers are bleeding money. They print less of my first editions every year. Maybe they're trying to hint that an old lady like me should retire. Ha-ha, I'm just joking. Ignore me.

O? I worked with him at his old job, when he was

a literary editor. We've known each other for ages. It must be almost twenty years now.

But after only a few years, they transferred him to another department. What was it called, again? The horror one. That's right, it was the editorial department for the monthly magazine OOOO. I didn't hear anything from him after that. They didn't have the budget to hire me. Ha-ha.

But we started working together again after he changed publishers and wound up back as a literary editor. Well, you know, this field is pretty small. Connections mean something.

Oh, that's right. You're looking into ●●●●●, aren't you? Is this for OOOO? Is it still a monthly publication? What? They're only making one-offs now and then? Wow. I guess we all have it rough.

Um, what were we talking about again? That's right, ●●●●●.

Have you read any of my books? You have? Thank you.

That'll speed things up. As you know, I write a lot of horror.

I'm so grateful that I've been able to do this for so many years.

So this was about, oh, twenty years ago. O was still a newbie; he'd just started doing proper work as a literary editor, and he took over working with me from his predecessor.

While O and I were discussing my next project,

I received an offer from an editor working in children's literature.

They wanted to make a compendium of horror stories for children, centered around the theme of school, and they didn't want to pull any punches. That was why they hired me, an actual horror writer.

O and I had been thinking of making my next piece something about the propagation of rumors.

So I decided to explore how elementary school children spread horror stories, then use that to gather material for the children's book.

In the end, however, the piece with O moved in a different direction, so the materials I gathered didn't help much with that project. The book turned out wonderfully, though, so pick it up if you're interested.

Oh, sorry. Forget about that for now. I had never written a children's book and knew absolutely nothing about children, so I decided to do some field research.

The editor for the children's book used his network to connect me with three elementary schools in the Kanto and Kinki regions, and O and I went to interview the students in person, just the two of us. We could have brought the other editor, but three's a crowd, you know.

One of those schools was in ●●●●●.

By the way, do you believe in ghosts? Yes. I see.

Me? Well, this may surprise you, since I'm a horror author, but I don't.

Now, this is just my personal opinion based on my many years as a horror writer, but I believe that ghosts are born from human fears.

Ghost stories don't come from people who have seen a ghost with their own eyes.

If an anatomical model was dancing every night in some elementary school's science room, it would be huge.

Think about it. That kind of room is a dedicated space, separate from the other classrooms. It's usually in a special building or annex. Fewer people go there, and less often. And when someone visits a place like that, they get scared, even if it's only a little. The fact they're not sure what's scaring them just makes the experience even more terrifying. So in order to share that vague, ominous feeling, they make up a ridiculous story like the one about the dancing model.

I used a location in that example, but it could be anything that elicits fear.

There's a theory that the *jinmenken*, or human-faced dog, that got popular a little while back was a response to children's fears about stray dogs.

Of course, it's perfectly fine to be scared of stray dogs. But some kids have dogs as pets, so they're not afraid of strays, and they don't understand the other children's fear. The *jinmenken* helped them find a shared target for their fear. Maybe that's why it spread so fast once the media picked it up.

Just like the *jinmenken*, certain fears are shared

by people all over Japan. That's why the ghost of a girl named Hanako haunts school bathrooms across the country, and why people see ghosts in every hospital morgue. The same process produces them all.

But at the same time, as such collective fears survive through the ages, their names and details can change.

No one has a landline anymore, so Mary, the haunted doll, calls your cell phone. Sometimes she even sends an e-mail. Maybe she's not even called Mary anymore, but the vague fear of communicating with someone whose face you can't see has survived.

That's one reason so many horror stories involve mountains, rivers, and oceans, no matter what era they're from. Humans fear forces of nature they can't control, and that fear persists, passed down under different names through every age.

But there are exceptions.

If something deeply shocking happens in a small area, it can become a scary story unique to that region. And that's precisely what happened at that elementary school in ●●●●●.

There are two sections in my *Scary School Stories* series that came from interviews I conducted in ●●●●●. One is in *The School with Nine Mysteries*, and the other is in *Scary Stories from Around the School*.

That's right. Those are the ones. I remember the work fondly. You've already read them, I see.

Originally, I didn't plan on publishing those two stories, but the first and second books sold well enough to keep the series going, and to be honest, I'd pretty much run out of scary stories based inside schools. That volume expanded into the areas around schools. Of course, by the time it reached the printers, it had been a while since I'd done my research.

The interviews I conducted at ●●●●● weren't like those at the other schools.

A local incident a couple of years prior had influenced the scary stories there.

For *The School with Nine Mysteries*, I interviewed several students, then summarized the stories that seemed common to all of them.

Seven of them were typical, the kind you hear everywhere. But all the children ended with the same two legends.

That struck me as odd, so I asked about it, and they told me the last two stories had gotten popular at their school recently. You see, that school originally had only seven mysteries, too. But then two more cropped up, making nine.

The new stories were *The End-of-Day Bell* and *Akio*.

In addition, the students told me two more stories that took place outside of school. Both of those were recent, too. They were the basis for *The Jumping Woman* and *Akito and the Phone Booth*. Actually, there was one more. But I couldn't include it.

It was exhilarating. I was witnessing firsthand

how elementary schoolers spread scary stories—the very subject of the book I intended to write.

As I just mentioned, I believe scary stories emerge from vague, undefined fears. At the time, I spent countless hours trying to determine the underlying fear that had given rise to the stories in ●●●●●.

I discovered an incident where a mother and son committed suicide.

I have copies of the newspaper articles from when it happened. They were inside the notepad I used for my research. Being organized is helpful at times like this. Here you go.

The boy who died was an eleven-year-old named Akira ○○. Yes, you write his name with the character 了, the same one that means "end."

The article doesn't mention the mother, but she killed herself one year after Akira.

I tried asking the students, but they said their parents forbade them from talking about Akira's death, and they refused to discuss it. So did the teachers, of course. But I found out the school bell really does ring a few minutes late sometimes.

So O and I started asking around the neighborhood. We made up some excuse to talk to housewives on their way home from the grocery store. O was good at that kind of thing.

Coincidentally, one of the people we interviewed had witnessed the incident with Akira.

She lived in an apartment close to the elementary school and was just coming back from shopping when it happened. As the school bell rang to signal the end of the day, she was pushing her bicycle loaded with groceries up the hill to the apartment. She could see a group of people gathered in the park inside the complex.

A child was hanging from a tall tree in the park.

Below him, she could see a woman she assumed was his mother screaming his name, half-mad, with her arms in the air, jumping to try to get him down.

The kids had just gotten out of school, and a bunch of them had gathered around to watch.

The woman we interviewed ran over and told one of the kids to get an adult, then ordered the others to go home. She didn't want them to witness such a gory scene.

The mother kept jumping and wailing until a police car and an ambulance arrived. When they took down her child, all the life had drained from his face.

The police took the mother to the station. No elementary school-aged kid could hang himself from such a tall tree without a platform, and there was no platform. Eventually, though, the newspapers labeled it a suicide.

Someone else provided us with additional details, this time about the mother.

The family at the center of the incident lived close to the elementary school.

The father passed away soon after the son was born, so the mother and child were the only ones living in the house.

She was very friendly, if a little weird, and neighbors whispered that she was part of some weird religion. But she never caused any trouble.

After her son killed himself, people who ran into her around town said she seemed very depressed, which is understandable.

A couple of months later, though, she started acting strange.

She would appear in town, excitedly talking to anyone she saw.

The magazines and talk shows on the subject seemed to find the suicide explanation dubious, and they raised various other theories, such as murder, bullying, and abuse. Because of that, the other people in town felt sorry for the mother and continued to interact with her.

But sometime after that, she started putting up strange sticker-like talismans on the walls and windows of her house. One day, a neighbor stopped by with the local circular, and when she opened the front door, they could see that the wall, floor, and ceiling were completely covered with them.

When the mother ran out of space in her house, she started sticking the talismans on telephone poles and community bulletin boards around town. Eventually, she started just handing them out to people walking down the street.

She'd say things like "A great discovery!" or "Blessings upon you!"

She'd completely lost her mind.

Not too long after, she was found hanging in her house.

If you remember, I mentioned that one story didn't make it into the books.

That was the story about her house.

After the woman died there, the house became abandoned. Locals started calling it the Talisman House, and rumors circulated that it was haunted by a female ghost in a red coat.

The child's mother had often worn a red coat.

Naturally, I couldn't include anything about a vacant house that's still standing. Even if I wanted to, the story would be too similar to real events, and that would cause an ethical problem.

So I shelved it.

I think the mother was probably the inspiration behind the *Jumping Woman* story that wound up in the book.

I didn't include this detail, but all the kids said that the Jumping Woman wore red clothes. So both the clothes and her jumping resemble the mother.

I debated whether to include the story about Akira, too. But after talking with O, we decided to go ahead with it. I changed the name to Akio or Akito and left out the part about him killing himself.

* * *

I have a little more information about Akira, too. Adding it to the nine mysteries would have made things unnecessarily complicated, so I separated it out into another story.

All the rumors said that Akira was offered to *Mashiro-san* as a sacrifice.

Yes, yes. That very same *Mashiro-san* mentioned in the nine mysteries.

I think that one's based on the horror story called *Cow Head*. It's one of those stories where anyone who finds out what the monster looks like dies, so no one knows the exact details. And the horror repeats itself.

One of the kids I interviewed said that, according to his older brother, Akira died as a sacrifice. *Mashiro-san* found another student, and they made Akira take their place.

That might be what started the rumors about Akira killing himself because of bullying.

Oh, one more thing. More than one student from that elementary school killed themselves.

According to what I heard, there was another student besides Akira.

That death was buried in the local papers and never received the same level of attention as Akira's. That was partly because another major story at the time overshadowed it, and party because it was more obviously a suicide.

A girl jumped to her death from the roof of a

building in the same complex where Akira killed himself. It happened a couple of years after Akira's death. Sometimes one suicide can trigger another, you know.

Does she have a scary story about her? No, she doesn't.

There weren't a lot of witnesses, so people didn't talk about it as much.

But people say she killed herself because she became friends with Akira, and he ate her.

It seems strange to say he ate her when she died of suicide. But rumors are just like that, I guess.

Following Akira's death, the story I called *Akito and the Phone Booth* spread, and people say the girl who killed herself called Akira and made a wish.

If a scary story emerged every time someone died, then we would expect the number of school mysteries to increase in tandem. Instead, like what happened with *Mashiro-san*, it makes more sense for the new story to get blended into a more familiar one. But the one about Akira wound up becoming its own thing.

I mostly stayed true to the information I got from the students about Akira and his mother, but I did exaggerate some of the details.

If the witnesses really all went missing, then who's telling the tales? Ha-ha.

That's all I know about ●●●●●.

What do I want from you? Yes, well… I said I wanted ideas for my next project, but the truth is, there's nothing I want to ask you.

I came here to warn you, as a fellow writer.

O shared some of the details with me. There are scary stories about ●●●●● told all over Japan. Some people have died. It sounds like the mother and child I just told you about are somehow related.

If that's true, then this is quite a frightening story.

No, I'm not saying I doubt you.

That's not what I mean. It's a matter of perception.

I still don't believe in ghosts. But I don't want to hear anything more about this case.

The reason? It's simple. Because I don't want to change my worldview.

If you tell me something that makes it obvious ghosts exist, then I won't know how to handle them in the future.

Let's say that ghosts, or something like them, are really out there. At the very least, they're definitely harmful to humans. Maybe they're like the coronavirus.

What if, as soon as they gain a foothold, they start attacking randomly, with no sense or logic to their actions? Some people might escape, but others will die.

If it turns out ghosts are like that, then I've spent my whole career putting my readers in danger.

And I can't accept that. I refuse to let that be the case.

So, with that in mind, I want to give you a warning.

Listen to the ramblings of this old lady.

If you don't believe in something, it's as if that thing doesn't exist.

I don't believe in ghosts.

But you think that ghosts are involved in this thing you're investigating, right? And you want to uncover the truth.

What I was doing—looking into the roots of elementary school horror stories—is the same as what you're doing. But our objectives are different.

Take my advice and stop.

As the old saying goes, "Ghosts are nothing but wilted pampas grass."

If this ghost turns out to be nothing but wilted pampas grass, what a relief that would be. But what will you do if it turns out to be something else?

When I looked into it, this story of the Jumping Woman and her child turned out to be simple rumors born from a shocking incident where a mother and son committed suicide. That was the pampas grass masquerading as a ghost, and I found it. But what are you trying to find?

…So you're not going to give up?

Okay. Well, if you're that determined, then I won't stop you.

* * *

In that case, I'll tell you one more thing.

To be honest, I know a family that died at the dam in ●●●●●.

This was six or seven years ago. And it was murder.

The husband worked as a designer at one of my publishers. He was still young, but he created wonderful work, and he even designed some of my book covers. He lived in Nagano, but we got on well and would have dinner together whenever he came to Tokyo.

Apparently, he pushed his wife and daughter off the side of the dam.

The police conducted a thorough investigation, but ultimately labeled it a murder-suicide, concluding that he killed his wife and daughter but couldn't go through with killing himself.

I don't believe that at all. He loved his wife and daughter deeply.

He and his wife spent years trying to get pregnant but never could. They discussed adoption and eventually took in a little girl. They loved her as if she was their own—maybe even more. He often showed me pictures of her. She was very cute.

I'm a single old lady, but hearing him talk about her, I started to think of her as a sort of grandchild. He kept saying he would bring her along the next time he came to Tokyo…

Sometimes weird coincidences happen. But it was

still a coincidence. That's how I view it, anyway. I'll let you come to your own conclusions.

…By the way, what about you? Are you married? Oh, so you're single. Many people are in this industry. I'm not one to talk, of course.

What? Oh, I see. You're divorced. That's pretty common these days.

Are you eating enough? It's hard when you live alone without anyone to take care of you. It sounds like you're not. Your complexion is pale, too. You can't buy all your meals at convenience stores, you know. Thinking about horror stories all day must be depressing. I know someone who's really nice.

Oh, sorry. I'm overstepping. When you're my age, you get nosy.

Transcript of an Interview 4

Excerpt from S's files—*About the Stone 3*:

Man: Some of my questions might make you uncomfortable, but I'd like you to tell me everything you know.

Woman: I told the police and the reporters everything I can, so there's not much else to say. I heard the place was already shut down.

Man: I'm here to talk about more than just the incident. I'm an editor at this magazine.

Woman: Huh? Um… What do you want…?

Man: As you can see, my magazine covers the paranormal. Please don't get offended. It's just that I heard a strange rumor about the retirement home you used to work at.

Woman: Strange, like something supernatural?

Man: Yes. But I'm not covering the deaths just for entertainment. I want to show my readers the truth.

Woman: Oh, I knew it. I knew what happened wasn't normal.

Man: Did anything strike you as odd?

Woman: Yes. But I didn't think anyone would listen to me. And I don't believe in ghosts, either, so I never said anything.

Man: I see. Naturally, I will keep your name and information confidential, so would you tell me what you noticed and how you felt about it?

Woman: Okay… Where should I start? How much do you know about the incident?

Man: Just what the media reported. That some Alzheimer's patients and a staff member from the retirement home were involved in a mass suicide.

Woman: That's right. First, though, I need to correct you on something. The patients who died didn't have Alzheimer's. The news called it a retirement home, but Tokoshie Space was classified as a general care home.

Man: I see. My apologies. What is a general care home?

Woman: Essentially, it's a facility for elderly people who are still healthy and active. The residents there didn't have Alzheimer's or any other major issues. Some people worry about living by themselves at that age, even without any heath conditions. So places like that simply offer support services to help them live their lives.

Man: I see. That's good to know.

Woman: I only worked there for three months or so, though.

Man: Why did you choose to work at Tokoshie Space?

Woman: My husband was transferred to Kanagawa. I decided to get a part-time job, and one day I saw a Help Wanted ad. The facility had just been built, so they were probably looking to expand their staff. My mother is also getting older, so I applied thinking the job might help me care for her one day. And you don't need a nursing certificate to work at a general care home.

Man: How did you like it there?

Woman: It was a really nice environment. Nursing facilities are extremely physically and mentally demanding, but the residents at a general care home more or less take care of themselves. So it was fine. Well, there were a few things I had to get used to, but the other staff taught me everything I needed to know.

Man: How could a mass suicide happen in a place like that?

Woman: I think it had something to do with that thing.

Man: That thing…? Are you talking about a stone, by any chance?

Woman: Yes, that's right… I knew it.

Man: Would you tell me more?

Woman: That…stone…sat in Tokoshie Space's recreation room. There was a TV, so people would hang out there. Sometimes they used the space to hold events. It was a weird stone. It was big, black, and rough, and it was set on top of a platform.

Man: Did it look like some kind of religious object?

Woman: No, nothing like that. It was like a piece of art or some kind of ore. We had some landscape paintings in the reception lounge, so I figured the director liked art. And none of the residents' family members seemed bothered by it.

Man: But it looked strange to you?

Woman: Yes. Because having it there was kind of dangerous. It's heavy. We were supposed to avoid anything that could hurt residents if they fell, so it didn't make sense to me.

Man: That sounds like a very reasonable concern.

Woman: I hesitated to say anything because I was new, so I didn't do anything about it. But other strange things happened.

Man: Like what?

Woman: Some of the residents would face the stone and engage in odd behavior.

Man: What sort of odd behavior?

Woman: All kinds of stuff. My job included planning and holding recreational activities during the daytime. Things like group origami events and light exercises like ring toss. None of the activities were required, but some residents never signed up for anything and focused all their attention on the stone. They stared at it with their mouths hanging wide open, or walked up to it and bowed, or surrounded it and raised their hands in the air. Some of them even jumped up and down.

Man: That didn't worry the other staff?

Woman: No. And that's strange, too, right? But it was a busy place, so they might not have had the time to worry about it. And even though none of the residents had Alzheimer's, the mind still starts deteriorating with age, so I tried to not let it bother me too much.

Man: Was there anything else?

Woman: I once saw another staff member jumping in front of the stone with the residents. Even if they were just playing along, I thought that was going a little too far. That was when I finally asked a coworker about the stone.

Man: Did they know anything?

Woman: It's hard to say. They said that the facility director had placed it there. I asked where it came from, and they said it was a special wishing stone that had been enshrined on a mountain in ●●●●●. That sounded really creepy to me—like some kind of cult thing. I wondered if they were trying to prey on a susceptible elderly population to gain followers.

Man: It certainly is an unnerving story. Did anyone ever ask you to join a group?

Woman: No. Nothing. But I never brought up the stone again after that.

Man: Was there anything aside from the stone?

Woman: Yes. When we had art sessions for recreation time, we'd always choose a theme. It was supposed to help prevent dementia. But some residents completely ignored the theme and drew a weird image.

Man: What did they draw?

Woman: They filled page after page with the same drawing of a torii.

Man: Did they ever say anything about it?

Woman: Yes. They all said the same thing. That they were looking for the person who would stand underneath it…

Man: That's creepy, all right.

Woman: There were other things. I heard this from someone who started working there right around the same time I did. We didn't talk much because I worked the morning shift and she worked evenings. But one day between shifts she told me something really bizarre.

Man: What was it?

Woman: At night most people are asleep. But she said she heard some weird voices coming from a few of the rooms. Actually, they were more like screams—high-pitched shrieks and low moans. She hurried over, but they stopped when she opened the door, and she found the residents sitting up, staring ahead blankly. Another time, she heard people chanting something like a Buddhist invocation.

Man: Which invocation?

Woman: I don't know. I only heard about it secondhand. But she said the voices were crisp and clear, not mumbled like people usually do when they pray.

Man: She didn't go to a supervisor?

Woman: Of course she did. But the director just said that some people moan or get confused in their sleep, and not to worry about it. That sounded dubious to her, and what with the stone and all, I found it downright spooky.

Man: Pardon me for being blunt, but did anyone ever die outside of that incident?

Woman: Yes. Three people passed while I was working there. I heard they all died peacefully from old age, without any other possible cause. I don't know if three is a lot—it is a facility for the elderly, after all—but what really unnerved me was that all three of them were obsessed with that stone. I made the connection after the third person died, so I cut back on my hours and started looking for another job.

Man: Were you still working there when the incident happened?

Woman: Technically. I hardly spent any time there by then. And it happened during the night.

Man: Would you mind telling me anything you know about it?

Woman: I wasn't there, so this is all hearsay. Someone on the night shift discovered four residents and a staff member lying spread out on the floor in front of the stone.

Man: How did they describe it to you?

Woman: The media called it a mass suicide, but I heard the whole thing was really bizarre. They all voluntarily hit their head on the stone and died with their head covered in blood.

Man: That's…

Woman: I said a staff member was involved, but they didn't commit suicide. Apparently, the four residents grabbed them and smashed their head against the stone before taking turns bashing their own skulls and killing themselves.

Man: No one else working that night saw or heard them?

Woman: The other employees said they didn't notice a thing. They went looking for the staff member when they didn't come back from their rounds, and they found all five of them lying on the floor.

Man: That's pretty hard to believe.

Woman: Right? Could four elderly people really overpower someone like that? And why do it to begin with? The only thing I can think of is all of them were obsessed with that stone. The staff member they murdered was the same one who jumped in front of it.

Man: Did you mention that to the police?

Woman: No. I didn't want to get involved. But as I'm sure you know, the police run thorough investigations with strange incidents like this one. In the end, they labeled it a mass suicide resulting in a murder, then declared the matter closed. And they don't release details of sensitive cases like this to the media. The daytime talk shows seized on it as a springboard to focus on issues involving elderly care, but they only talked about it in light of greater social issues and didn't cover the actual incident itself.

Man: As a reporter, I'm afraid I know how that goes… By the way, because I approached you for an interview, I feel obligated to tell you how I got this information on the stone. Would you like to hear it?

Woman: No, thank you. I don't want anything more to do with this. Let sleeping dogs lie and all.

Man: That's understandable. Thank you for your time today.

About a Place in the Kinki Region

4

Ozawa called me out of the blue one day, and I went to meet him at a café in Jinbocho.

We sat down and waited for our drinks. Once they'd arrived, he drained his iced caffe latte and started talking.

"Will you listen to my theory?"

I decided to hear him out.
After laying out his theory on the mountain caller, he continued.

******

The red woman and a boy showed up in *Scary School Stories* by the horror writer XXXX, who I interviewed. Not just any boy, though, Akira.
That interview cleared up most of the root causes behind everything except for the mountain caller. What a tragedy.

The Talisman House from that thread I found online must have been the same house where the red woman and Akira lived. The talismans have all been peeled off now, though. I feel like the periodic thumping the original poster described shares some similarities with the red woman's MO.
Your follow-up interview with the man who did his thesis on the cursed

video showed that while the red woman haunted him for a while, she later left him alone, and Akira replaced her. If they're family, that would make sense.

As I mentioned before, unlike the mountain caller, the red woman actively seeks people out. It's like she wants to be found. And Akira is probably somehow involved.

I can't believe she sent letters to my work when she was still alive.

Well, I don't know exactly when she killed herself, so I'm just speculating. The letters all give off the general impression of being written by someone still in possession of most of their faculties. The author was simply a little deranged, is all.

It was the third letter that made me suspect they had come from the red woman. I recognized that phrase, "Thank you for finding me." She most likely sent the letter to another reporter from our publisher who investigated her child's suicide. Other departments write gossip columns like that, such as the illustrated weekly journal OOOO, which spawned the monthly magazine OOOO.

As he was working on *Scary School Stories* and XXXX's new book, O must have been asking around the company, trying to find anyone who had interviewed people about the suicide in ●●●●●. Someone from a different department heard about that and gave him the mother's letters, which then ended up in the pile of research materials where I found them.

A different department published it, so I haven't found the back issue with that article. But I'm still looking.

They probably pressured the mother into giving an interview and then wrote something that painted her in a bad light. That would make the red woman a victim in this case.

Speaking of victims, Akira is one, too.

The horror writer said that Akira served as a sacrifice to *Mashiro-san*, which I think means he became like the sacrifices in that game the kids in the apartment complex played, *Masshiro-san*. The mother found him, and then they became yet another supernatural entity.

According to the interviews, *Mashiro-san* has existed for a while as one of the school's seven mysteries. If we go far enough back, I bet there's a story somewhere about *Mashiro-san* calling people over to the mountain. That became the basis for the game called *Masshiro-san* that the apartment kids played. The game's role in Akira's death led to further rumors spreading about him and his mother, the red woman. That's what I think, anyway.

However, the mountain caller and Akira both share one strange feature. Both open their mouths wide and ask for a sacrifice.

Strictly speaking, no direct testimony states that the mountain caller opens its mouth wide, but one of the letters to the editor and *Ghost Photo* mention something to that effect. I think the image of the gaping mouth is somehow related to the mountain caller. But Akira in the *Akito and the Phone Booth* story opens his mouth wide, too.

Both phenomena also involve sacrifices, but they seem to have a slightly different significance. The mountain caller usually receives dolls, while the sacrifices in the *Masshiro-san* game include inorganic objects and sometimes the lives of animals or other people.

In Akira's case, the sacrifice was his life. It seems he had no choice but to offer it up if he wanted to be forgiven.

In terms of differences, the mountain caller seems to have clear objective, while Akira's motives are more vague. It seems as though he wants to steal the lives of others. Perhaps he wants to consume them, like it says in *Scary School Stories*.

If he's taking the life of a human being, he might consume their life force, then have them throw their physical bodies off the apartment building's roof, like how the mountain caller influences people to jump off the dam. That's one way to explain it, anyway.

In addition, Akira himself follows the targets he haunts, just like the red woman. This is also different from the mountain caller.

* * *

Based on these ideas, Akira, who died because of the mountain caller, inherited certain features from it, but ultimately became a different phenomenon.

Both the horror writer's testimony and the letters mention that the red woman was interested in spirituality when she was alive.

The thread on the Talisman House claimed that some items related to New Age beliefs had been left behind in her home, and it seems like she didn't own a Buddhist altar. The post on the medical consultation website also said "Thank you for finding me" and used that weird turn of phrase "Please guide everyone from a higher place."

This red woman is trying to spread something related to Akira in accordance with some specific ideology. Either that, or she's trying to make as many people as possible aware of Akira's existence. Using that sticker with his name, 了, is one way of doing that. Or at least that's what I think.

Just like Akira, the red woman is somehow connected to the mountain and the mountain caller in some way.

The woman who started the thread on the medical consultation website said her son went to the ruins of some corporate retreat. It might have been the same facility west of the mountain where the events in *The Truth Behind the Mass-Hysteria Incident at the School Camping Trip* took place. She didn't specify the exact location, but as you know, that place is famous for paranormal activity. Plus, it's the only big, abandoned facility in the area.

Cheating described how to summon *Mashiro-sama*, and those actions remind me of the red woman. I don't know when this game to summon *Mashiro-sama* started at that elementary school, but it's possible the kids who saw the red woman jumping frantically to get Akira down from the tree incorporated her movements into the *Mashiro-sama* summoning ritual. But if that's true, then it would reverse the relationship between the two stories.

And then there are the sticker and the strange letters to the editorial department…

******

Ozawa spoke in a flurry, as if possessed, without regard for my reactions, denying me any opportunity to interject.

When I eventually interrupted him, he finally stopped talking, took a deep breath, and said:

"I'm close. I can feel it. There's still a lot of unknowns, but I feel like I can just about connect everything together. This special edition is going to be spectacular."

He continued, the excitement never fading from his voice.

"I've come this far. I think it's time to visit ●●●●● for myself."

Of course, I tried to stop him.

But he went anyway.

Two months later, he was dead.

They found him in ●●●●●.

Dear readers, I'm so sorry for deceiving you.

This is where *About a Place in the Kinki Region* ends.

Published in August 2000
in a Certain Monthly Magazine

Heresy in the Country, an Undercover Report on a Cult

Do you remember the cult in ●●●●● that we covered in 1996?

We ran several exposés on cults around Japan following a terrorist act carried out by a religious sect the year before. Our magazine brought to light the truth behind a wide array of groups, from emerging religions to devil worshippers, and this cult was one of the ones we discussed.

Here's a quick review.

Spiritual Space, a fairly new religion, was established in 1991 and differs from typical belief systems in that it has no central figure.

Unlike Buddhism, Shintoism, or Christianity, they do not worship any deities. These women worship the universe itself.

I say *women* because every devotee of this religion is female.

Women come from all over to gather near the base of a mountain in ●●●●●, out in the middle of nowhere with nothing else around but a dam. Some women essentially live on-site.

They train and engage in meditation and yoga to bring themselves closer to the Truth of the Universe.

One of our sources, however, provided us with some disturbing rumors.

Reports of worshippers taking their own lives. Entire families committing suicide.

For our last piece, one of our editors paid the area a visit hoping to gain insider access for a special report. But the group's defenses were much tighter than anticipated, and the their PR manager gave our male editor a standard introduction in the reception room without allowing him to set foot inside.

Now, four years later, we decided to try again. Having learned from our previous mistakes, this time we sent a woman to go undercover and get the story.

Concealing her true identity as a reporter, she sneaked in as a lowly devotee to talk with other followers and learn the shocking truth behind this organization. This is her report.

******

I arrive at the train station a little past noon. In the car sent to retrieve me, the driver, a Spiritual Space devotee, tells me about the group.

Each member fulfills a clearly defined role, such as driver, publicist, office worker, or management staff.

While a handful of people act as leaders, there is no hierarchy within the group, and everyone addresses one another as equals.

The number of people in the congregation fluctuates between thirty and fifty. All are women, and some even have spouses and children.

We arrive at Spiritual Space, where the sheer size of the facility surprises me.

It feels like a small hotel. There is a lobby, meeting rooms, a large shared bath, a dining hall, and plenty of rooms filled with beds. The facility could house a very large group. In fact, many people seem to live here most days of the year.

In the reception room, a PR woman tells me about the group. I know most of this already, but I listen attentively to show her my potential as a serious initiate.

She explains the cost of joining—that is to say, the group's revenue stream—and surprisingly they have no rules about how much worshippers must contribute, instead letting each person pay what they can when they can afford to do so. When I ask how they manage to maintain such a large facility without a fixed contribution, she replies that a few very wealthy members keep the place running. It's worth investigating further, but I doubt she'll say any more to a newbie like me.

A woman I assume is a leader gives me a tour as she tells me about the facility, then I join some other devotees in a meeting room for yoga.

We do mostly standard poses like cat and moon, but there are some unique ones. For those, we raise our hands in the air. When I ask why, they tell me that lifting your hands toward the sky helps you receive the cosmic energy that will open your chakras.

Next, we meditate. Staying silent in such a large group feels uncomfortable. I just pretend to meditate and get a headache for my trouble. Who knows, maybe my chakras are opening.

The yoga and meditation are called training, but they're completely voluntary, and we can spend the time outside of our assigned roles as we see fit.

The group feels kind of like a female-only club, except it's a cult.

I chat with a few other worshippers during my free time to learn more.

They're all friendly, actively practicing the group's teaching that a gracious heart guides one to the universe. They start each conversation by thanking the other person. I actually find their friendliness unsettling.

I first speak with a middle-aged woman, probably in her fifties.

When I ask about family, she tells me she has a husband and a teenage son. Curious, I inquire further and discover they all get along quite well and her family supports her spending half the week attending to her religious activities.

Only women can join the group, but men can proselytize, so her husband and son help her go out and recruit new members.

Frankly, I don't understand the mindset of someone who would preach a religion denied to them, even if a family member was deeply involved.

Their preaching apparently consists of handing out pictures on the street or sticking them up in conspicuous places. They have no scripture, so I wonder if those pictures serve as their recruiting tool. I ask to see one, but the woman says she needs to attend to her cleaning work, so I miss the chance.

The next person I speak with is a young woman in her twenties.

A bright smile on her face, she starts talking before I have the chance to probe her reasons for joining.

"I think I'll be able to go to a higher place soon."

She continues, though I'm visibly confused. According to her, it's an open secret that there are two types of followers: those who can go to a higher place and those who can't.

I ask what will happen when she goes, and she replies, "I'll gain the Truth of the Universe."

When I press for details on what that means, her answer makes little sense. But the strange look in her eyes terrifies me.

I have yet to see any sort of brainwashing in the group's activities. Their lives seem free and unrestricted. Even so, I have to question why these people have all gathered to worship here.

The last person I talk to is a woman around forty.

She has been a devotee since the group's founding. She lost her elementary school–aged son the previous year and is training diligently to meet him in this higher place. It dawns on me that this group offers a kind of sanctuary for people with wounded hearts.

She sobs openly, lamenting that even with all her training, she still hasn't made it to the higher place, and I feel pity for her.

I momentarily forget my mission and encourage her to continue training while cautioning her against doing anything rash in order to see her son again.

* * *

Before I know it, it's time for dinner.

Those living off-site all go home, and those who stay file into the dining hall to eat.

There, everyone talks and enjoys their meal.

I can't eat much, though. Everything is tasteless.

The food from the kitchen looks no different than any other meal, but it lacks any flavor whatsoever. Is that because it's not seasoned well enough? No one else seems to mind, but I leave most of my plate untouched.

After dinner, the PR woman calls me into the reception room again and asks if I'd like to join.

Naturally, I say yes, hoping to gain more information for this story.

With a satisfied look, she thanks me, then she informs me I can observe a ritual accessible only to followers.

She leads me to a different area of the building.

We pass through two sturdy-looking double doors to find more than ten worshippers in a dimly lit room.

A peculiar scene presents itself.

In the center of the room, a wooden platform supports a large stone decorated with a sacred rope.

On each side of the square platform, a hunched worshipper devoutly writes something on a paper placed on the floor.

I assume this is the picture that woman in her fifties mentioned. A quick glance over one woman's shoulder reveals an image with the character 女 written on it.

The other devotees form a circle around these bowed worshippers as they draw, repeating eerie, bizarre movements.

They jump, hands raised high.

Everyone keeps repeating some gibberish.

The following is a transcript of a secret recording I made.

"Ruki emashiramu dojie uzume"

"Meshi taga haha aoemashiraoizu memi ochikudo"
"Zogi tsumashirafuie hamo sumo ooe"
"Airuzu mesomashiraudzu jiemifu oporeru tozue"
"Doiishimashirame koyoi asu pikuso"
"Suei mikururu ruemashiraoki munashi"
"Aoie fuzumodzui seromashirao aburuiso"
"Chimemi fuzuroite tottusumo iteto bunaru mashira ike komiteru"
"Fueo iepushi mashira"
"Rimashiratsu fuitoto mina oi oerutsu"
"Mashira shikoe ributsui tote mizu"

For a while, I stand frozen, observing the ritual.

I ask the calmly smiling PR woman at my side to escort me out of the room, then ask her what it was all about.

She informs me that the women were training to reach a higher place and to guide everyone from above.

Because Spiritual Space has no central person or object of worship, the stone in the center of the room acts as nothing more than a medium to reach a higher place.

They draw pictures next to this stone, which harnesses the universe's power, then use those pictures to save those who find them.

The devotees engaged in that strange dance around the stone, jumping with their arms raised, simply say whatever comes to mind in order to channel power through the stone.

Even assuming that is all true, the sacred rope on the stone clearly comes from Shintoism. I press her for more details, but she only repeats that the stone is special.

Hearing her story makes me feel woozy. Not figuratively, but literally woozy.

I let her know I don't feel well, but she expresses no concern.

Sensing an imminent danger to myself, I say I need to use the restroom, then call my editor from a private stall.

I lose consciousness just as I hear the siren of the ambulance my editor called for me.

******

Our reporter was admitted to a nearby hospital but thankfully suffered no major complications and returned home safely. She fell ill again after submitting her report, however, and is currently still hospitalized.

We contacted the group, suspecting that some drug might have been slipped into her food. But the phone number no longer worked, and the group's website had disappeared.

We sent a writer living in Kansai out to the facility, but the buildings were empty, and they could not find the large stone mentioned in the report.

Japan is still home to scores of dangerous, hidden cults.

Each approaches regular people with a smile, but their true motives are to brainwash or steal. We here will never stop working to expose the dark side of these cults, to ensure the tragedy of five years ago is never repeated.

Transcript of an Interview 5

Excerpt from S's files—*About the Stone 4*:

Man: Hello.

Woman: …Hello.

Man: I'm a reporter researching the local geography for a report on ●●●●●. Can I give you my business card?

Woman: …Sure… Oh, I think I've heard of this publisher. The address is in Tokyo. Why are you all the way out here?

Man: I'm planning on writing a book. May I ask you some questions? We can just talk like this.

Woman: Okay, sure.

Man: Thank you. There's a shrine on that mountain over there. Has it been there for a long time?

Woman: Oh yes. I think it's pretty old. A priest used to live there, but he passed away a couple of decades ago, and it's been empty ever since. They used to have a summer festival with food stalls and everything when I was young. But that was almost fifty years ago. I haven't been there since I was in school. I'm Buddhist, anyway.

Man: Did they have any other festivals besides the summer one?

Woman: What? Well, let's see. Oh, I think they used to do something in early May for Children's Day, too.

Man: I see. Do you know what kind of god was enshrined there?

Woman: Oh, what was it…? I think it was a god to ward off evil spirits, but I don't remember all that well. Sorry.

Man: …It's okay. Do you know if that god has any connection to a stone?

Woman: A stone? Oh, you mean *Mashira-sama*? I know that one. It's not the god of the shrine, though. That one is in a smaller *hokora* on the shrine grounds.

Man: Really? The stone was in the empty *hokora*? And it was called *Mashira-sama*?

Woman: What do you mean, empty? *Mashira-sama's* stone should still be there.

Man: I didn't see a stone. There were a lot of dolls, though…

Woman: Impossible. The stone has to be there.

Man: Somebody might have taken it.

Woman: Who would do something as immoral as that?

Man: Do you have any idea who might want to take it?

Woman: I don't know… Oh, what about them? That group was always doing strange things. Everyone always gossiped about them because they kept wandering around the mountain.

Man: What group is that?

Woman: A long time ago, someone built a facility near the mountain for some sort of religious group. Apparently, some strange people did lots of weird things up there.

Man: Are they still there now?

Woman: They're long gone. The buildings were repurposed for a corporate retreat, but they're abandoned now.

Man: Would you mind telling me a little more about this religion?

Woman: Oh, I don't know anything about it. They were really peculiar, so everyone in town left them alone. No one around here would know anything.

Man: …I see. Do you remember what they were called?

Woman: Oh, that was decades ago… It was an odd name… Something Space or Space Something, I think. I don't really remember.

Man: Thank you. I'll see what I can find out. By the way, can I ask you about the *Mashira-sama* enshrined in the *hokora*?

Woman: Sure, but you certainly ask about some strange things. I heard the story when I was just a girl… *Mashira-sama* is a monkey god.

Man: A…monkey?

Woman: That's right. A big white monkey. When we were little, our parents would scare us by saying that *Mashira-sama* would kidnap us to make us his bride if we wandered around at night. Some of the older people who really believed in him would go up there and leave persimmons as offerings when they were in season.

Man: Persimmons?

Woman: Yes, the fruit. You know them, right? Apparently, monkeys love them.

Man: Were persimmons the only thing people offered?

Woman: Oh, that's right, they left something else, too. Dolls. Old women would leave handmade dolls. There's a big staircase leading up to the shrine, right? It was probably good exercise for them.

Man: I see… Dolls.

Woman: They relocated a lot of people out of the area when they built the highway near the dam, and that decimated the population. There used to be lots of houses around, but hardly anyone lives here anymore. So no one remembers *Mashira-sama*.

Man: Have you ever seen this *Mashira-sama*?

Woman: Oh, you foolish little boy. Have you ever seen the Buddha? *Mashira-sama* is just a myth.

Man: No, I meant *Mashira-sama's* stone.

Woman: Oh, that. Yes, when I was little. It's a craggy black stone that's almost big enough to be a small boulder. I remember asking my mother why it wasn't shaped like a monkey.

Man: What did she say?

Woman: Something like… Oh, well, you know. I don't think she really knew. You're really curious about *Mashira-sama*, aren't you? My mother has passed on, but my father is still around. He's in the house now. Would you like to talk with him?

Man: Really? Yes, I'd love to.

About a Place in the Kinki Region

4

"I need to talk with you."

Ozawa sounded a little upset over the phone.
As requested, I went to a café in Jinbocho to find him waiting for me. When I sat down, he thrust a piece of paper at me.

"Read this."

I did as he asked.
It was an undercover report about a cult in ●●●●●.
Before I could finish reading, he asked:

"You wrote this, didn't you?"

His words caught me off guard.
It was a reasonable question. I'm a woman, after all.
When I first started out as a freelance writer, I had to take anything I could get, so I wrote some pretty extreme articles.
I remember being hospitalized around that time.
But I don't remember writing the article in question.

I denied it, but Ozawa wordlessly indicated the last part of the article.
The author's credits listed my pen name.

* * *

"You have a unique pen name. If you didn't write this, then who did?"

I fervently denied ever writing that article.

I could see the doubt in his eyes as he continued.

"So, what? You were in some sort of fugue state at the time?"

Just as he finished the sentence, he seemed to realize something.

"It couldn't be…"

I urged him to continue.

"The women in *New UMA Discovered! The White Man!* and *Waiting* didn't die. Every woman who lived either lost their memory or succumbed to something like Alzheimer's… What if that happened to you?"

Uncertain myself, I couldn't respond.

"But if that's true, then why were you saved? Why are you still alive after infiltrating their group?"

My barely functioning brain raced. Why am I still alive? Why wasn't I chosen as a bride? Why couldn't I go to a higher place…?

Then it struck me.

The undercover report was from 2000.

I could never forget. I lost my son just one year earlier.

He died in a traffic accident.

Following that, my husband and I decided to separate, and I quit my job at a publishing company to start freelancing.

I had always assumed that the intense physical and psychological stress of working too hard had landed me in the hospital. But according to the article, it was because of what happened at the facility.

If I really was the author, then it made sense that I would forget my assignment and console that other woman in the group.

Based on that idea, I offered Ozawa a theory.

The mountain caller targets women who have never given birth.

We had assumed it targeted young women indiscriminately, but it seemed this mysterious entity selected its targets very carefully.

Ozawa remained silent for a moment before replying.

"You could be right. No, that's probably it. I'm sorry for doubting you."

I told him not to worry and that he didn't need to apologize, then we ordered our drinks.

Black coffee for me and an iced caffe latte for him.

He fidgeted constantly while we waited for our drinks to arrive.

Once they came, he drained his before talking.

"I'm scared," he began. Then he told me the following:

******

I realized something while reading that article.

The worshippers' chant matched the one from the club my friend told me about in college almost perfectly.

There were some minor differences, though.

But how and why do I know that?

I just heard about it from a friend, so how do I perfectly remember the words they were chanting?

And how did my friend remember a barrage of random words muttered simultaneously by multiple people after only hearing it once?

Some friends contacted me the other day. Female friends.

They asked me to stop calling them in the middle of the night and talking nonsense.

They claimed I called them and said the following:

* * *

"Let's go to the mountain. It'll be fun. Let's go."

I don't remember making those calls.

But when I checked my call history, I had contacted a bunch of women in my address book in alphabetical order.

Thinking about it now that I've heard your theory, I didn't call anyone with children.

Have I lost my mind?

I think about this special edition all the time, no matter what I'm doing.

At first, I thought I was just really excited about my first assignment. But I realized something in the shower the other day when I looked in the mirror. My reflection was smiling.

I'm enjoying this.

And that scares me.

What about you?

******

He continued, not waiting for my reply.

He expounded his opinion on the mountain caller, the red woman, and Akira.

When I eventually interrupted him, he finally stopped talking, took a deep breath, and said:

"I'm close. I can feel it. There's still a lot of unknowns, but I feel like I can just about connect everything together. This special edition is going to be spectacular."

He continued, the excitement never fading from his voice.

* * *

"I've come this far. I think it's time to visit ●●●●● for myself."

I had no right to try to stop him.
Because I was no longer safe, either.
So he left.

Two months later, he was dead.
No, it would be more accurate to say that's when they found his body.
The editorial department called me to say they couldn't reach Ozawa.
Knowing he was no longer alive, I told them he might have jumped off the ●●●●● dam.

I heard they found his drowned corpse, along with that of a woman he didn't know.
Both of them were smiling.

Dear readers, I'm so sorry for deceiving you.

This is where *About a Place in the Kinki Region* ends.

Transcript of an Interview 6

Excerpt from S's files—*About the Stone 5*:

Elderly Man: You want to hear about *Mashira-sama*? That's a bizarre thing to be looking into.

Man: Yes. Wait…what do you mean, bizarre? *Mashira-sama* is a god, right?

Elderly Man: That thing, a god? Wait, is that what my daughter called it?

Man: Yes, she did. She said it's a monkey god.

Elderly Man: Of course she did. I'm the one who told her that. All right, young man, listen up. I don't mind talking about this, but don't tell anyone or publish anything about it, okay?

Man: I understand. I'll keep this confidential.

Elderly Man: He's no god. He was just a regular man.

Man: A regular man?

Elderly Man: Yes. His name was Masaru.

Man: They enshrined a regular man and erected a *hokora* for him?

Elderly Man: It was the only way.

Man: Was a stone involved at all?

Elderly Man: …Where should I start? I first heard it from my father, who heard it from his father, so the story comes from when my grandfather was alive. Around the Meiji era. Did you know that this entire area was a big village before they built that dam?

Man: Yes. I knew that.

Elderly Man: Well, everyone knows everyone else out here in the country, so it's like a big family. But one house, Masaru's, was a little strange. I wouldn't go so far as to say that they were outcasts, but everyone kept their distance from that family.

Man: Why?

Elderly Man: A bear killed Masaru's father when he was a little boy, so it was just him and his mother. But she was frail and bedridden.

Man: Then Masaru was taking care of her?

Elderly Man: Apparently so. Unlike his mother, Masaru was strong, and he worked hard in the fields. But he changed after his mother died. He started acting a little odd.

Man: Odd, you say…?

Elderly Man: Maybe he was lonely. His mother required all his time and attention, so he never showed up for town meetings and was still single in his twenties. He stayed home all the time and started making dolls, then talked to them all day long like they were his wives.

Man: Didn't anyone in the village do anything?

Elderly Man: Everyone worried about him, of course. They decided an actual family would bring him back to his senses, so they arranged meetings for him with women in the village. But it didn't work.

Man: Why is that?

Elderly Man: Well, you see… Let's just say he was a little strange… It seems he was a difficult person to spend time with.

Man: …Okay.

Elderly Man: Some villagers teased him from time to time. Young man, do you know the Persimmon Tree Code?

Man: Sorry, no.

Elderly Man: That's okay. Young people these days wouldn't. Basically, it's a symbolic dialogue newlyweds use on their wedding night. People still used it when I was a boy.

Man: What do you mean, a symbolic dialogue?

Elderly Man: The man asks, "Do you have a persimmon tree?" Then the woman answers, "Yes, I do. And there are some persimmons on its branches." The man then says, "May I have a persimmon?" To which the woman replies, "Yes, help yourself." Of course, there doesn't have to be a persimmon tree. The exchange is just a way to confirm consent.

Man: I see. That's interesting.

Elderly Man: So we used to have this custom, and someone, half joking, told Masaru about it, saying he would find a bride if he just asked girls if they had persimmons.

Man: And did Masaru do it?

Elderly Man: No, he misunderstood and pestered every woman in the village, telling them, "I have persimmons. Come with me."

Man: …Oh.

Elderly Man: It upset everyone, and none of the women would go near him after that.

Man: What a sad story.

Elderly Man: …It is. Well, one night a woman living near Masaru was murdered. Someone split her head open. The villagers searched for the murderer and found a big black rock with blood on it in Masaru's fields. No one knew how the rock got there, and it didn't look like the kind found in these mountains. When they discovered it, the murdered woman's husband and some young people in the village surrounded Masaru and beat him up.

Man: …Oh, wow. Did Masaru really do it?

Elderly Man: Probably. He confessed when the people interrogated him.

Man: Did they kill him?

Elderly Man: No, they had beaten him senseless, but he smashed his own head against the stone he used to kill that woman and died.

Man: That's horrible.

Elderly Man: Apparently, his face looked horrific at the end. His mouth and eyes were wide open.

Man: What happened after that?

Elderly Man: They buried him in the mountain forest, saying they didn't want him in the village cemetery. Then they placed the rock on top as a kind of tombstone.

Man: And that's the *hokora*?

Elderly Man: No, no. After they buried him, women in the village started dying. It was very strange, but they all died after smashing their heads on that rock. Some people started saying Masaru must have called them.

Man: So it was Masaru's curse?

Elderly Man: Everybody seemed to believe so. They quickly built a *hokora* by the shrine on top of the mountain to placate him. But they didn't have an image of worship to place inside. So they took the stone, wrapped a sacred rope around it, and called it *Masaru-sama* when they prayed to it.

Man: …And did that appease Masaru?

Elderly Man: …Apparently. People started offering him the persimmons and dolls he had obsessed over in life.

Man: I see. But why is it called *Mashira-sama* now?

Elderly Man: Well, they couldn't tell such a horrible story to children. But they had to keep making offerings to Masaru. So they created a monkey god with a similar-sounding name and passed down the legend over the generations. I also used *Mashira-sama* when I told my daughter about it.

Man: …Thank you so much for this. I think I understand now.

Elderly Man: I'm sure my daughter told you, but the shrine is completely run-down these days. The gods do horrible things when they are forgotten. I pray for my ancestors every day in front of our house shrine.

Man: …But Masaru wasn't a god.

Elderly Man: Young man, think about it. If the people around you start praising everything you do, then you start feeling special, chosen, even if you don't deserve it. It's the same thing. If everyone worships and fears something, then that thing becomes a god. And then to be gradually forgotten? Gods, Buddha, monsters, they all cease to exist if no one knows about them. So they assert their presence when they feel that people are forgetting. That's just how it is.

Man: I see. Thank you so much for the story… I'm very sorry to have to ask this, but is everything you just told me true?

Elderly Man: …What do you mean?

Man: I went to the shrine and I saw the *hokora*

with the missing stone. But it was about as old as the main shrine. And it was all wood. Just like the main shrine, I didn't see any nails holding it together, either. It looked like it had been made by skilled carpenters with experience in building shrines. Nothing about it seemed hastily constructed.

Elderly Man: Why are you asking that now? I don't know anything about that. I heard the story from my father. Are we done? It's almost time to eat.

Man: My apologies. Thank you for your time.

Signboard with the Shrine's History

Excerpt from S's files—*About the Stone 6*:

●……●…Shrine

The history of…
This shrine is………according to………called……
…………built in……year…………
This…god………………is………secr………………
…details…unknown………, ……legends……from……
……, fell……heaven………, demon………eat……………
………calms……………curse………………
………May 3……calm………festival…………

Notes for the article:
"Found this board in the bushes by the ruined shrine. Weatherworn and scribbled over, it was so damaged I could barely read it, but I wrote down the legible parts."

About a Place in the Kinki Region 5

I see you have read this far.

I'm so sorry.

I've been seeing them since my online meeting with Ozawa.

They whisper in my ear, saying, "Write everything. Spread it everywhere."

The whispers come to me in my dreams.

It seems I went too far.

Desperate, I made talismans in hope of finding salvation, but the whispers continued.

They only stopped while I was writing this.

Writing became my one way to survive.

I had to dive deeper into the curse, and I continued writing in order to escape it.

I know why it wants to grow, to spread.

Yet I continued writing, helping it spread to others.

I wanted to be saved. I wanted to live.

Even though it would make all of you sacrifices.

I knew Ozawa was dead, but I lied about looking for him so I could spread this curse.

Reading that my friend was missing piqued your curiosity and lured you in, kind reader. Even without that trap, masking the place's name behind ●●●●● spurred you to continue reading in the hopes of figuring out the real location. Perhaps you even wanted to talk about it online.

Unfortunately, I knew all this. As a writer, I know how to manipulate readers into spreading information.

At the beginning when I asked for your cooperation, I meant I wanted you to read this book.

But I kept some things from you.

That was the last piece of my conscience. My way to resist.

The stronger your connection to a horror story, the more its curse affects you.

So I ended the story several times.

Then you, reader, wouldn't have to touch upon the curse anymore.

But it didn't allow me.

No matter how many times I ended the story, the whispering did not stop.

Not until I wrote everything, spread everything to others.

She chose me because I was the same.

Giving the work to someone in a similar situation let her spread the curse more effectively than any talisman.

By "the same," I mean someone who is also a mother.

She went house by house, not in search of children but in search of mothers.

She wanted a woman who would sympathize with her. A woman fit to raise a child with her.

I had lost the child I gave birth to. I had sympathized with others at the facility. I must have been the woman whose experiences most closely resembled her own.

Foolishly, I pulled at that once-severed connection and got involved with her again.

She despised the media. At the same time, she knew firsthand the influence it wields.

She knew a freelance writer like me was the best choice to spread and grow her child.

That woman, the red woman, wanted to resurrect her son.

She clung to the fake god who spurned her, even though she believed in it. What's more, that god took her child's life. She didn't even understand the implications of what she was doing.

She is a helpless fool who kept praying, even when she could see her dead son hanging in front of her.

She is beyond pitiful.

Stealing the stone and changing the talisman's characters to her child's name let her revive something, but that something only resembled her child.

Still, she believed it truly was her son.

So she co-opted the curse and used the talismans to infect innocent people, all in order to raise something that only consumes other people's life force.

She morphed into a horror herself, repeating the same actions even after losing her soul.

But that still wasn't enough.

So she used me.

Beings like her have no soul. They merely hunt their prey on instinct.

Even as she wrote that the god she'd worshipped was false, she never shed a tear.

That is just how such beings are. Human reason doesn't apply to them.

But that woman is not the only pitiful one.

If we trace these events back in time, that man—even the child—were simply sacrifices.

Sacrifices demanding more sacrifices. How ironic.

The demon is still out there, sucking the blood of humanity and birthing more false gods.

But knowing that makes no difference now.

This is truly where *About a Place in the Kinki Region* ends.
There is nothing more to write. I have written everything.
Knowing ●●●●●'s precise location is pointless.
Reader, you are already intricately linked to it.
It is too late.

I no longer hear her whispers.
Maybe she has forgiven me.
But I see a boy, standing there in the corner of the room, watching me.
Make of that what you will.

Dear readers, I'm truly very sorry.
And thank you for finding me.

了

Source Materials

This is the missing person poster for K that the police made. Ozawa found it posted on a horror-related thread on the internet. Some people black out her face because they believe it will appear distorted.

Letters to the Editor 1

A drawing included with the letter from the reader who was being followed by a strange man. The disturbing picture was created with harsh and erratic lines. Could it be depicting the grinning man with a gaping mouth mentioned in the letter?

A picture found in the interview data for the February 2015 edition of the magazine, which included the short story *A House to Rent*. The writer who interviewed A probably took this photo of the actual piece of paper from the copier mentioned in the story.

Letters to the Editor 2

I KEEP REPEATING MYSELF. BUT YOU ARE NO GOOD.
YOU. CRUEL AND ARROGANT
LIKE MY OLD NEIGHBOR SAID YOU ARE HARMFUL
YOU KNOW THAT MICROWAVES ARE DANGEROUS TOO.
DON'T YOU
I HAVE BEEN A RECEPTOR FOR A LONG LONG TIME BUT
YOU DO NOT HAVE THE EARS TO LISTEN
YOU DON'T EVEN TRY TO RECEIVE IT BEFORE IT
IS TRANSMITTED AS ELECTRICITY. HOW UTTERLY SINFUL
THOSE DEEP BELOW THE GROUND ARE CRYING IT'S
SUCH A SHAME.
AND THEY STILL SWIM THROUGH THIS WORLD LIKE
TUNA NOT AWARE OF ANYTHING
WEARING HUMAN SKINS WITH WIDE SMILES ARE
THEY IMITATING SAINTS?

BUT PRETENDING TO BE HUMAN THEY HAVE LOST
EVERYTHING INSIDE OF THEM LONG AGO
THE WEST WAS NOISY AGAIN YESTERDAY THE
SOUND RANG IN MY EARS LIKE THE HOWLING
OF MONKEYS
AND THEY DO NOTHING. BUT KEEP WATCH AS A
GROUP!!!!
CHILDREN ARE ALWAYS ADORABLE. THEY HAVE TO BE.
YOU KNOW THAT, RIGHT
YESTERDAY THE NOISE FROM THE CALCULATOR STOPPED
AT 9 IN TWO DAYS' TIME, THEY MIGHT PRESS 10
THAT'S HOW FAR IT'S SPREAD
WE MUST KILL THE EVIL OUR MASTER SAYS SO
AKIRA IS EVIL THAT WOMAN BIRTHED IT
BUT NOT FROM HER WOMB THE DEMON, GAVE IT
POWER SUCH A SHAME

FROM FAR AWAY. IT USED ELECTRICITY TO ATTACK AND
TORTURE PEOPLE THEN YOU SPREAD YOUR RUMORS
AND NOW IT'S OVER
THE BEAUTY OF A BIRD SOARING IN THE SKY IT'S
GLORIOUS!YOU CAN'T DO THAT WITH BATTERIES
ALL THE FOOD CONTAINS POISON TOO. IT DOES
THAT CREATURE IN THE MOUNTAIN ONLY A
SHAMELESS FOOL WOULD CALL IT A GO.D . ITS
POWER MADE IT A FALSE GOD
GO BE TRICKED BY PERSIMMONS AND THINGS IF
YOU CHOOSE
THE BAD ONE IS THE DEMON

The undated letter from an unknown sender.
The words don't make sense, but the letter seems like some kind of warning.

Yet I know what it means.

IMG_0053

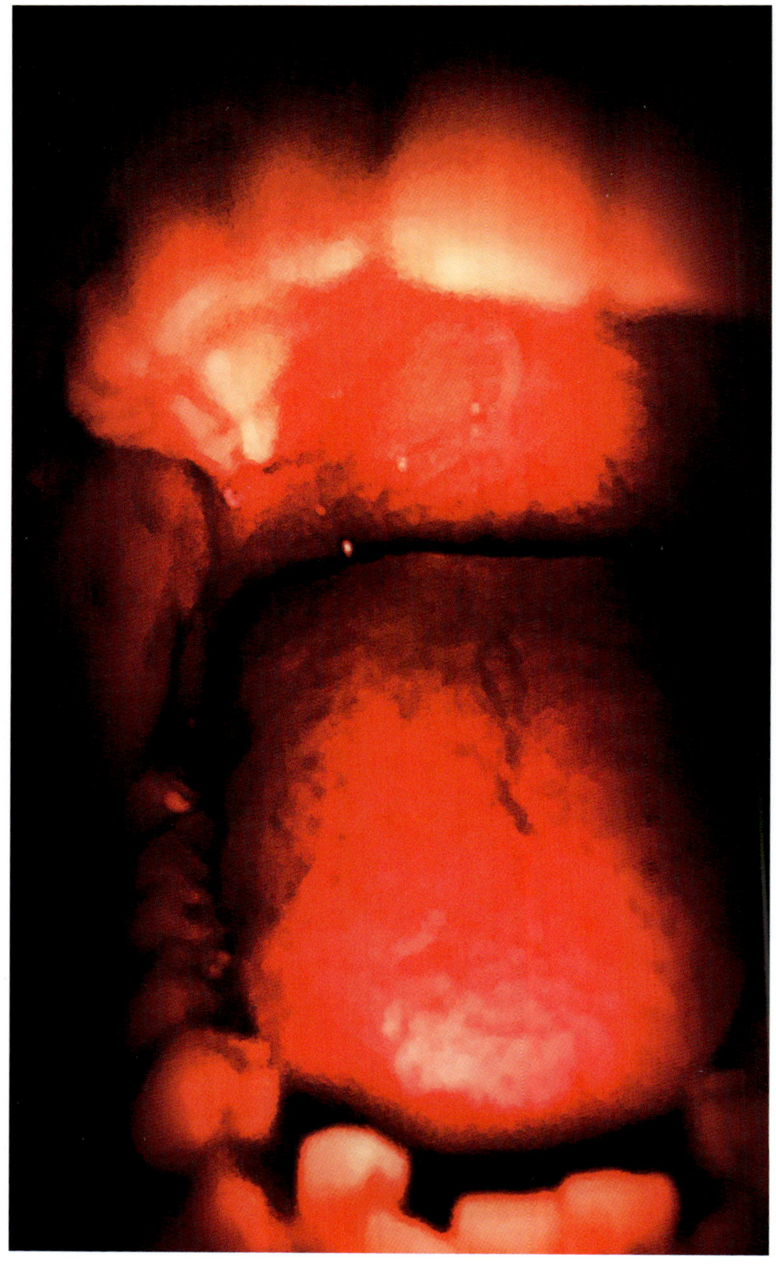

Waiting with an open mouth

A

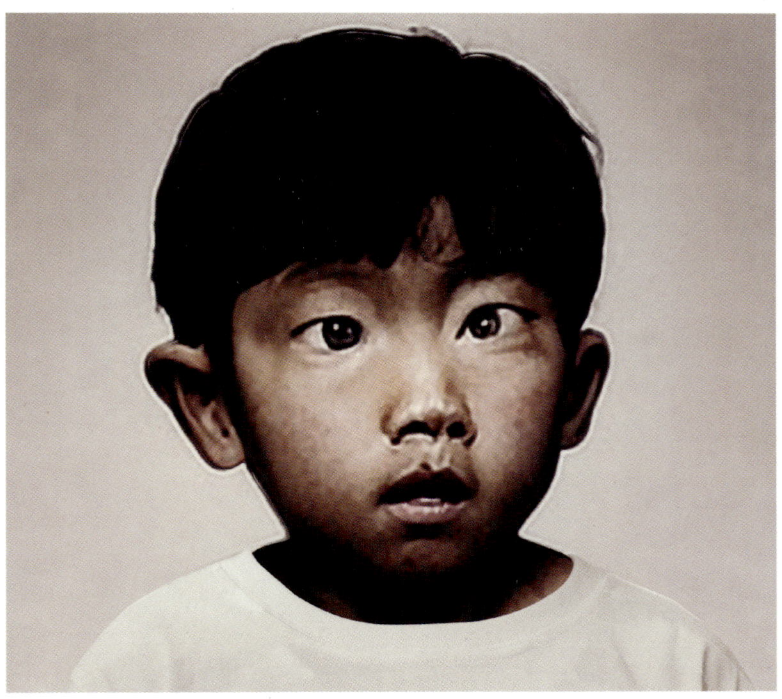

Akira

He's watching